GREAT STORIES IN E

MORE TALES FROM SHAKESPEARE

Abridged and Simplified by
S.E. PACES

S. CHAND
AN ISO 9001: 2000 COMPANY

S. CHAND & COMPANY LTD.
7361, Ram Nagar, New Delhi-110 055

S. CHAND & COMPANY LTD.
(An ISO 9001 : 2000 Company)

Head Office: 7361, RAM NAGAR, NEW DELHI - 110 055
Phones : 23672080-81-82; Fax : 91-11-23677446
Shop at: schandgroup.com
E-mail : schand@vsnl.com

Branches :

- 1st Floor, Heritage, Near Gujarat Vidhyapeeth, Ashram Road, **Ahmedabad**-380 014. Ph. 27541965, 27542369..
- No. 6, Ahuja Chambers, 1st Cross, Kumara Krupa Road, **Bangalore**-560 001. Ph : 22268048, 22354008
- 152, Anna Salai, **Chennai**-600 002. Ph : 28460026
- S.C.O. 6, 7 & 8, Sector 9D, **Chandigarh**-160017, Ph-2749376, 2749377
- 1st Floor, Bhartia Tower, Badambadi, **Cuttack**-753 009, Ph-2332580; 2332581
- 1st Floor, 52-A, Rajpur Road, **Dehradun**-248 011. Ph : 2740889, 2740861
- Pan Bazar, **Guwahati**-781 001. Ph : 2522155
- Sultan Bazar, **Hyderabad**-500 195. Ph : 24651135, 24744815
- Mai Hiran Gate, **Jalandhar** - 144008 . Ph. 2401530
- 613-7, M.G. Road, Ernakulam, **Kochi**-682 035. Ph : 2381740
- 285/J, Bipin Bihari Ganguli Street, **Kolkata**-700 012. Ph : 22367459, 22373914
- Mahabeer Market, 25 Gwynne Road, Aminabad, **Lucknow**-226 018. Ph : 2226801, 2284815
- Blackie House, 103/5, Walchand Hirachand Marg , Opp. G.P.O., **Mumbai**-400 001. Ph : 22690881, 22610885
- 3, Gandhi Sagar East, **Nagpur**-440 002. Ph : 2723901
- 104, Citicentre Ashok, Govind Mitra Road, **Patna**-800 004. Ph : 2671366, 2302100

Marketing Offices :

- 238-A M.P. Nagar, Zone 1, **Bhopal** - 462011. Ph : 5274723
- A-14 Janta Store Shopping Complex, University Marg, Bapu Nagar, **Jaipur** - 302015, Phone : 0141-2709153

© *Copyright Reserved*

All rights reserved. No part of this publication may be reproduced, stored in a retrieval system or transmitted, in any form or by any means, electronic, mechanical, photocopying, recording or otherwise, without the prior permission of the Publisher.

No one is permitted to publish a key to this book without the written permission of the publishers.

ISBN : 81-219-2265-8

PRINTED IN INDIA

By Rajendra Ravindra Printers (Pvt.) Ltd., 7361, Ram Nagar, New Delhi-110 055 and published by S. Chand & Company Ltd., 7361, Ram Nagar, New Delhi-110 055.

CONTENTS

Chapter	Page
1. As You Like It	2
2. The Tempest	22
3. Macbeth	38
4. A Midsummer Night's Dream	59
5. Julius Caesar	78
6. Othello	95
7. Questions	119

INTRODUCTION

William Shakespeare (1564-1616) is usually considered the greatest dramatist the world has known, as well as the finest poet who has written in the English language. No other writer's plays have been produced so many times in so many countries, and no poet's verse has been read so widely in so many lands. His works have been translated into more languages than any book in the world except the Bible. However, little is known of his life. His birthday is generally given as 23rd April, 1564. He married at the age of 18 and become a well-known actor and playwright by 1592. Between the years 1589 and 1611, he wrote at least 36 plays, 2 narrative poems and many sonnets. He retired a wealthy man and died in 1616.

Charles Lamb (1775-1834) was a well-known English essayist and critic. He and his sister, Mary Ann Lamb (1764-1847), became famous when they rewrote and simplified Shakespeare's plays so that children, as well as adults, could read and enjoy them. In this book, six of the most famous tales are totalled in simple English. Generations of readers have found these stories highly interesting. If you enjoyed reading "Tales from Shakespeare", you will also enjoy reading this book.

AS YOU LIKE IT

The People in the Story

Duke Senior : King

Duke Fredrick : Duke Senior's brother

Rosalind : Duke Senior's only daughter.

Celia : Duke Frederick's daughter.

Charles : A famous wrestler

Orlando : Son of Sir Rowland De Boys and a nobel youth

Oliver : Orlandos' brother.

Sir Rowland De Boys : A friend of Duke Senior

Ganymede : Name used by Rosalind when she disguished herself as country a lad.

Aliena : Name used by Celia when she disguished herself as a country girl.

Adam : Orlando's faithful servant

AS YOU LIKE IT

1

ROSALIND AND CELIA

Duke Senior ruled his country wisely and well, but his cunning brother *Frederick* seized his dukedom from him. The duke had to flee for his life. He fled to the *Forest of Arden*. There he lived with some faithful followers who gladly shared the exile of their master.

The duke and his company lived contentedly in the peaceful forest, for they loved the simple care-free, open-air life there. In the forest they had no enemies but winter and rough weather. The duke's only regret was that his only daughter *Rosalind* was not with him. She had been kept behind at the court of Duke Frederick who wanted her there as a companion for his own daughter *Celia,* Rosalind's cousin. Rosalind and Celia were very fond of each other. The two girls were happy together although Rosalind grieved over her father. She missed him very much. Celia knew this and did her best to comfort and to cheer her cousin.

2
THE WRESTLING MATCH

One day, something happened which quite changed the lives of the two girls. There was a wrestling tournament at the court. *Charles,* a famous wrestler, had come to display his strength and skill. He wrestled with three brothers and defeated them all easily, one after the other. Then, still fresh and smiling, he was ready for his fourth opponent.

This was a noble and handsome youth, much younger than Charles. The girls pitied him instantly and begged him not to wrestle. "Charles is an usually strong fighter. He will kill you," they told him. "You have no chance of winning. Don't risk your life!"

"Ladies, I thank you for your kindness," the young man replied. "Let him kill me. It doesn't matter, because I have no friends to grieve over my death."

He spoke so sadly that Rosalind was filled with pity. "I have but little strength," she told him, "but I would add that to yours." The young man smiled gratefully at her. Then he turned away from the ladies to face Charles, the champion wrestler. The match began.

3

ORLANDO

The young man had spoken the truth. He had no friends and even his own brother *Oliver* was his enemy. *Orlando,* for such was his name, was indeed unfortunate. His father, a close friend of Duke Senior's, had died when Orlando was very young. He had left the boy in the care of his elder brother Oliver. The latter had treated Orlando cruelly and had given him no schooling. In spite of this, Orlando had grown into a noble youth, the image of his noble father. Everybody praised him. This made Oliver angry and envious.

Oliver had gone to Charles before the wrestling match. "My brother Orlando," he had told the champion, "is an evil fellow. He looks noble but he is, in fact, the wickedest creature on earth. He is even plotting to murder me. If you break his neck, I shan't mind. You'll be doing the world a good service. If you don't, you'll regret it, for he'll find some way to kill you sooner or later." Charles had believed these false words. "I shall have no mercy on him," he had promised.

4

ROSALIND AND ORLANDO

Charles fought fiercely but Orlando won the match. He threw the champion to the ground so heavily that he lay there, unable to move or speak. Duke Frederick congratulated the new champion and asked him his name.

"Orlando, the son of *Sir Rowland de Boys*."

At that name, Duke Frederick turned red with anger. Sir Rowland, the friend of Duke Senior, had been his enemy. "I wish

that you had been the son of another father," he said in anger.

Rosalind had fallen in love with Orlando at first sight. She was delighted to hear that he was the son of her father's old friend. She took off the chain that she was wearing round her neck and placed it round Orlando's. "Noble youth," she said, "wear this for me, will you? I, too, am unfortunate." Her kindness and beauty won the heart of Orlando and he instantly fell in love with her.

5
IS BANISHED

Unfortunately for Rosalind, Orlando had to leave the court at once. It was dangerous for him to stay there when Duke Frederick was his enemy.

After Orlando had gone, Rosalind became silent and sad. Celia did her best to cheer her up but her efforts were in vain. Duke Frederick, who was angry with Orlando, was also angry with Rosalind who had openly shown her liking for the youth. For some time, the duke had been thinking of sending Rosalind away from his court. He felt that she was too popular with the people who pitied her for the loss of her father. Accordingly, one day, when Rosalind and Celia were talking about Orlando, he interrupted them with these harsh words.

"Rosalind, you must leave here instantly. If, in ten days' time, you are within twenty miles of my court, I shall have to kill you."

Both girls were shocked at this harsh and unexpected command.

"Why must I leave? What wrong have I done?" asked Rosalind.

"You are your father's daughter—that's enough," the duke told her.

Celia begged her father to let Rosalind stay with her, but he would not listen to her. He repeated his command and turned away.

6

FLIGHT OF ROSALIND AND CELIA

Celia loved her cousin too much to let her go away alone. "In banishing you, my father has also banished me," she told her. "I'm going with you. No one in the world shall ever separate us." The two girls decided to go to the Forest of Arden in search of Rosalind's father.

Celia, who had a practical mind, at once began to make plans for the journey. "It would be dangerous for us to travel in our fine dresses," she told her friend. "Let's dress like two country-girls. Then we shan't attract attention."

"We should be

safer still if one of us dressed as a man," said Rosalind. "I am taller than you. I will."

They disguised themselves as a country lad and girl, brother and sister. They also changed their names. Rosalind took the name of *Ganymede* and Celia that of *Aliena*. They took all the money and jewels they had and left the palace secretly.

7

ORLANDO FLEES WITH ADAM

Meanwhile, Orlando was on his way back to his brother's house. He was drawing near it when his faithful servant, old *Adam,* came out to meet him.

"Master! Master!" old Adam called. "Don't go home. Your brother is going to burn your room while you're asleep tonight. If that plan fails, he's going to try something else. He's determined to get rid of you. He hates you more than ever, since everybody is praising you for beating Charles. Keep away from his house. If you don't, it'll be your grave."

"But, Adam, where else can I go? I haven't any money I can't go about begging and stealing."

The good old man replied, "I've managed to save up five hundred

crowns. Take them—and take me as well. I know that I'm old but I'm still strong enough to serve you."

"O, you good old man!" cried Orlando whose heart was touched by such great goodness. "There are few like you in the world today. Nowadays men think only of themselves. Very well, we'll go together. I hope that we shan't need to touch your savings. I'm young and strong. I'll find work to do."

Orlando and faithful old Adam began their wanderings and, after a time, they came to the Forest of Arden where Duke Senior and his followers were living.

8

THE COUSINS' NEW LIFE

Rosalind and Celia found their way safely to the forest. The difficult part of their journey then began, for there were now no inns where they could buy food and shelter. They wandered here and there and were soon tired and very hungry. Rosalind was almost crying with exhaustion, but she remembered that she was a man. She then did her best to comfort and cheer Celia. They were almost fainting with weariness when they met two shep herds.

"Can you tell me where we can find food and lodging?" Rosalind asked them. "My sister is almost fainting with hunger and weariness. If you can help us, I shall pay you well."

"My master's house is nearby," one of the shepherds said, "but I don't know if you can stay there. He's selling it this very morning, and his sheep as well."

The kindly shepherd took the two girls to his master's house and gave them something to eat and drink. The girls then bought the house and the sheep, and kept the shepherd as their servant. They decided to rest for a while before going further to look for Duke Senior.

9
ORLANDO AND THE DUKE

All this time, Rosalind had not forgotten Orlando. She often wondered about him. Had he forgotten her? She did not know that he too had had to leave his home, and that he was now in the forest, not far away from her.

Like Rosalind and Celia, Orlando and his faithful servant lost their way in the forest, and they were almost dying of hunger.

Adam could go no farther. He lay down on the ground and begged his master to leave him there to die. Orlando carried him to the shelter of some trees and gently laid him down on the ground. "Rest here, old Adam," he said. "I'm going to find something to eat. I'll be back soon. Keep up your courage, old friend!"

Orlando ran off and by chance came upon Duke Senior and his band. They were eating their dinner when Orlando burst in upon them. Desperate with hunger, he drew his sword and shouted wildly, "Give me something to eat!"

Duke Senior answered him calmly, "Your manners are very bad, young man, but I can see that you are in distress. What's the matter?" Orlando told him about old Adam who was dying of hunger. "Go and fetch the good old man," the Duke said. "Bring him here and both of you shall eat your fill."

Orlando ran off and was soon back again, carrying old Adam. They ate till they could eat no more. Then Orlando told his story to the Duke. When Duke Senior heard that Orlando was the son of his old friend Sir Rowland de Boys, he was delighted. "Come and join my little band," he invited him. "You and old Adam are very welcome." Orlando and his faithful servant gladly agreed to join. That night they slept soundly, for their troubles were over.

10

POEMS ON TREES

What was happening to Rosalind and Celia in the meantime? Although they did not know it, their little cottage was not far from the Duke's camp. The two girls often took walks in the forest and they had come across a most astonishing thing. They had found the name ROSALIND carved on the trunks of several trees. This was not all. They had found verses pinned up under the name. These verses were all in

praise of the heavenly beauty of Rosalind, who had carved the name? Who had written the verses? Who was this unknown poet? Who was this unknown lover? It was someone who had known Rosalind before she had become Ganymede. But who? The girls thought and thought. In her heart, Rosalind hoped that Orlando was the man.

One day, Rosalind and Celia saw Orlando coming towards them with a companion. The girls hid themselves and overheard the conversation between the two young men. They heard Orlando's friend laughing at Orlando for writing verses to his Rosalind. Thus, they found out that the unknown poet and lover really was Orlando. How happy Rosalind was!

The girls came out of their hiding-place and spoke to Orlando. He did not recognise them and took Ganymede for a country-lad. Ganymede was soon teasing Orlando over his love for his Rosalind. "I know a cure for that," she told him, laughing. "Come and see me every day. Pretend that I'm your Rosalind. I'll soon cure you of your love."

Orlando went to see Ganymede every day, calling her, in jest, his Rosalind. He was happy with her. Rosalind was so happy with him that she forgot to look for her father. However, she met him by chance one day. He also took her for a country-lad. But he noticed that this country-lad was very much like his daughter.

"What's your name, my lad, and who are your parents?"

"My name is Ganymede, and my parents are as good as yours," Rosalind told him.

The Duke laughed at this bold answer, unaware that it was true.

11
RETURNING GOOD FOR EVIL

One day, when Orlando was on his way to see "his Rosalind"—as he always called Ganymede—he had a strange adventure. He came upon a man who was asleep under a tree. He went up to him. The man was in rags, dirty and unshaven. It was his brother Oliver! Never had Orlando expected to see his brother in the forest, and in such a miserable state. As Orlando looked, he saw that a deadly snake had coiled itself round his brother's neck. The snake was ready to strike. But Orlando's coming frightened it and it glided away into the bushes nearby. Orlando was watching the snake when he caught sight of a second deadly enemy. A lioness was crouched in the bushes, ready to spring on the sleeper as soon as he moved.

A dreadful thought came into Orlando's mind: "Let the lion-

ess kill Oliver. Why should I try to save him? He has always treated me so cruelly." Instantly Orlando drove this wicked thought away. He drew his sword and attacked the savages breast. He killed it but he himself was badly wounded in the struggle.

12
OLIVER REPENTS

The noise of the struggle awoke Oliver. He opened his eyes and he saw that the brother whom he had treated so evilly had saved his life. He had saved his life at the risk of his own. He was overcome with shame and remorse. He thanked Orlando with all his heart and begged Orlando to forgive him for his wickedness and cruelty. At once Orlando forgave him. From that day, Oliver was a different man and a truly loving brother.

Oliver had come into the forest to seize his brother because Duke Frederick had commanded him to do so. "If you don't bring him to me, dead or alive, you will lose all your possessions," the duke had threatened him. Duke Frederick meant to get rid of Orlando. But Orlando had saved Oliver's life, and so Oliver was no longer his enemy. He was on Orlando's side against the Duke.

Orlando had fainted from pain and loss of blood. As soon as he recovered, however, he sent Oliver with a message to Ganymede. He gave Oliver a blood-stained handkerchief to take with him. Oliver went to the cottage and told Ganymede and Aliena how Orlando had saved his life at the risk of his own. He told them how cruelly he had formerly treated his brother and how he now repented of his wickedness. He then showed the blood-stained handkerchief to Ganymede. When Rosalind saw how her lover's blood had stained the handkerchief, she nearly fainted. Then she remembered that she was a man and said that she was only pretending.

13

TWO WEDDINGS ARE ARRANGED

Oliver returned to Orlando. He had a lot to tell him. "Your friend Ganymede," he began, "nearly fainted when I showed him your blood-stained handkerchief. He said that he was pretending but I don't think he was. He looked as white as a sheet." Then Oliver added some surprising news. He had fallen in love with Aliena at first sight and she had fallen in love with him. They were going to get married as soon as possible. "We're going to live in the shepherd's cottage. You can have everything that I inherited from father."

Orlando rejoiced at his brother's happiness. "Let your wedding be tomorrow," he said. "I will invite Duke Senior and all his company. Go and tell Aliena to get ready for it."

Oliver left to carry the good news to Aliena. Then Rosalind came to see Orlando because she was very anxious about him.

She was happy to see that his wound was not as serious as she had feared. Orlando told her of the wedding that would take place the next day. He sighed deeply as he said, "I'm very glad that my brother is marrying the girl of his choice. Ah, how I wish that I could marry my lovely Rosalind!"

Rosalind knew that the time was near when she must stop being Ganymede and become Rosalind again. "If you wish to marry Rosalind tomorrow, you shall," she promised him. He looked at her unbelievingly and she then told him, "Believe me, I can make your Rosalind appear. I know a lot about magic. By the help of my magic, I can bring your Rosalind to you. "She spoke so definitely that Orlando had to believe her. "Put on your finest clothes," she told him, "and invite all your friends. If you wish to be married tomorrow, you shall, and to Rosalind, if you will."

14

AS YOU LIKE IT

The next day the Duke and all his followers were gathered together for the two weddings. Ganymede went with Orlando to the Duke and asked him, "If I bring your daughter here, will you let her marry Orlando?"

"I will. I would do so even if I had kingdoms to give away with her."

Ganymede then turned to Orlando.

"If I bring Rosalind here, will you marry her?" she asked him.

"I will. I would do so even if I were king over all kingdoms."

"Wait here then," replied Ganymede. She and Aliena then went behind a clump of trees. When they appeared again, they were no longer brother and sister. They were two beautiful girls, Rosalind and Celia, dressed in the fine clothes they used to wear

in court! All were dumb with surprise at the sight. When the girls told their story, everyone was filled with joy, especially Duke

Senior and Orlando.

Orlando married his Rosalind and Oliver married his Celia. Their weddings were followed by a great feast and all the forest rang with the revelry.

In the middle of the merry-making, a messenger came with good news for Duke Senior. "Your brother has given you back your dukedom," he told him. Then he went on to explain: "Frederick came to the forest with a large army, for he meant to kill you and everyone with you. But, on the way, he met a good old hermit and had a long talk with him. At the end of their talk, the duke became a different man. He saw the wickedness of his ways. He was ashamed and repentant. Now he says that he is going to spend the rest of his days in a monastery. He's giving the Dukedom back to you, and he's returning to your friends all the houses and lands he has taken from them."

And so the story ends, with everybody obtaining what he or she wished.

THE TEMPEST

The People in the Story

Prospero	:	A wise old man who was Duke of Milan, and a magician.
Miranda	:	Prospero's daughter.
Sycorax	:	A wicked spirit.
Ariel	:	A gentle and lively spirit.
Caliban	:	Son of Sycorax, and a monster.
Antonio	:	Prospero's brother.
King of Naples	:	Antonio's ally.
Gonzalo	:	A kind old man.
Ferdinand	:	Prince of Naples.

THE TEMPEST

1

PROSPERO'S ISLAND

Far away on a lonely island, there lived a wise old man and his daughter. The man was *Prospero,* a magician. The daughter was *Miranda,* a lovely young girl of sixteen.

They lived in a cave, one half of which was used as Prospero's study. It was here that he kept his books and studied magic most of the day. He knew so much of the art of magic that he was able to command the spirits of the island to obey him. These spirits obeyed him gladly because they were grateful to him for having rescued them from the power of the wicked *Sycorax* who had treated them cruelly. Indeed, at her death, most of them were imprisoned in the trunks of trees. Prospero 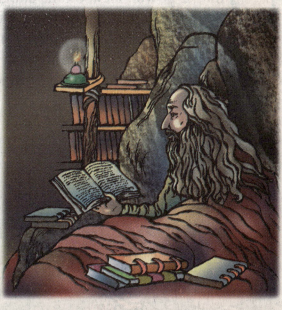 had freed them and so they served him willingly as their master.

The chief of these gentle spirits was *Ariel,* a lively little creature who was not only devoted to his master but also full of mis-

chief. To him, Prospero entrusted his most important tasks. One of these was to watch *Caliban*, a monster whom Prospero had found in the woods. Caliban, the son of Sycorax, was more like an ape than a man. Prospero had tried to make a man of him but Caliban's evil nature, inherited from his mother, had prevented this. Prospero therefore employed him to fetch wood and do the heaviest tasks. Caliban was lazy and disobedient and needed careful watching, but Ariel kept him in order and often played mischievous tricks on him. He would pinch and push the monster or, in the likeness of a hedgehog, block his path and frighten him.

2

FATHER AND DAUGHTER

One day, Prospero raised a fearful storm by means of his magic power. He took his daughter to the beach to watch a ship struggle against the wind and waves. The ship seemed likely to sink at any moment and those on board seemed likely to drown. Hearing that those on the ship were human beings, as she and her father were, Miranda was filled with pity.

"O, my dear father!" she cried, "if you have raised this dreadful storm, have pity on the people aboard the ship. Please don't let them drown. If I had the power, I would sink the sea below the earth in order to save those poor souls."

"Do not be anxious, my child," her father comforted her. "No one is going to be harmed." He paused and then went on, "It is for you, my child, for love of you, that I have raised this storm." Again he paused and then said thoughtfully, "You do not know who you are and where you come from. And you know nothing about me except that I am your father and live with you in this poor cave. Can you remember anything of your life before you came here?" he asked her. He did not wait for her to answer but added at once, "I think it's unlikely because you were then only three years old."

"I seem to remember something," Miranda told her father.

"What? Tell me all that you can remember."

"It's rather like a dream," began Miranda. "Perhaps I'm wrong....Didn't I have three or four women to wait on me?"

"You did, and even more. Strange that you should remember that. Do you remember how you came here?"

"No, sir," Miranda told him. "I can't remember anything else."

3

PROSPERO'S HISTORY

"Miranda," Prospero said gravely, "the time has come for me to tell you everything. Twelve years ago, I was *Duke of Milan* and you, my only child, were a princess. Even at that time my chief interest was the study of magic. I

spent most of my time in my study with my books. I left the government of my Dukedom to my brother *Antonio*. I trusted him but he turned out to be false and treacherous, as you will see. He plotted to rob me of my dukedom and he was able to do so with the aid of his ally, the *King of Naples*."

"Why didn't they put us to death?" Miranda asked.

"They daredn't do so openly because my people loved me. My cunning brother, however, put us in a rotten boat, without oars and sails, and pushed us out to sea. He thought that we should certainly perish. Fortunately, a kind old man named *Gonzalo* saved us. He secretly put in the boat water, food, and the things that I most prized, namely, my books on magic. Thanks to Gonzalo, we were able to reach this island of ours."

"O, my dear father!" cried Miranda, "I must have been a great trouble to you."

"No, my love," her father told her. "You were my little angel. You saved me from despair. Your smiles gave me strength and hope. From the beginning you have been my joy. I am never so happy as when I am teaching you."

"Dear father, I can never thank you enough."

"Now," Prospero continued, "I shall tell you why I have raised this fearful storm. On the ship over there are my enemies, my brother Antonio, and the King of Naples. They will be cast ashore and I shall meet them face to face. They will be in my power. They will be at my mercy."

"Prospero fell silent. He touched his daughter with his magic wand and made her fall asleep. Ariel had just appeared to tell his master what he had done with the passengers and crew of the ship. Miranda could not see Ariel or any other spirit. She would have been alarmed if she had seen her father talking to the empty air.

4

ARIEL REPORTS TO PROSPERO

"Well, my brave spirit, is all well?" Prospero asked Ariel.

"All is well," Ariel answered him. He described the terror on board the ship as it seemed likely to sink. *Ferdinand,* the son of the King of Naples, had thrown himself into the sea. His father had seen his son swallowed up by the waves and now he believed that he was drowned. "Of course he's safe," Ariel told Prospero. "I left him on the rocks, weeping for his father who, he thinks, is drowned. Actually, not a hair of his head is  harmed and his princely garments, although wet-though, look fresher than before."

"You have done well, my gentle spirit. Now go and bring the

young prince here. My daughter must see him." Prospero smiled at some secret thought and then asked. "Where is the King of Naples and my brother?"

"I left them looking for Ferdinand, though they do not think they can find him alive. The crew are all safe. The ship itself isn't damaged at all. I've left it far out at sea where it can't be seen."

"Well done, Ariel!" exclaimed Prospero. "And now I have something else for you to do."

"Something else!" exclaimed Ariel in dismay. "O, master! you promised me my freedom. I have served you faithfully. I've never told you a lie nor have I ever made a mistake. Can I not go free now?"

"Ariel, have you forgotten that wicked witch Sycorax? Didn't she shut you up in a tree where I found you howling? Didn't I set you free?"

Ariel, who was deeply grateful to Prospero, answered, "Pardon me, dear master, I shall obey all your commands."

"If you do, I promise you that you shall go free."

Prospero gave some other commands to Ariel. Ariel obediently flew off to where Ferdinand was sitting sadly on the rocks.

"Come, sir, follow me," Ariel commanded him.

The young prince was astonished at hearing a voice coming from the empty air but he obeyed. Ariel led him to Prospero, and Miranda who were sitting in the shade of a tree.

5

MIRANDA MEETS FRDINAND

Miranda saw Ferdinand first and could not believe her eyes. Except for her father, she had never seen a man before.

"What are you staring at, Miranda?" her father asked her.

"Oh, father, look at that beautiful creature!" Miranda exclaimed. "Is it a spirit?"

"No, child, it's not a spirit. It eats and sleeps just as we do. It's a man from the ship we saw. He's looking very sad at the moment but, all the same, you might call him handsome. He's wandering about looking for his friends."

Miranda had thought that all men had long white beards and serious faces like her father's. She was delighted with the sight of the handsome young prince. Ferdinand was astonished at finding so lovely a maiden in this wild and lonely spot. He took her for the goddess of the island. He called her a goddess.

Miranda told him, timidly that she was no goddess but a simple maiden. She was going to tell him more about herself when her father stopped her. He was very pleased that the two had fallen in love at first sight. All the same, he wanted to test their love by putting difficulties in their way.

Accordingly, Prospero spoke to Ferdinand harshly. "You are a spy," he told him. "You have come here to seize the island from me. Let me tell you that you won't succeed. I'm going to tie you up like a dog. The only food that you're going to get is shell-fish and roots." At this, Ferdinand drew his sword, ready to resist. But

Prospero waved his magic wand and fixed him to the spot where he was standing. Ferdinand was unable to move an inch!

Miranda was in tears. "Dear father," she cried. "Why are you so unkind? Have pity on him. He hasn't come here to harm us. I'm sure of that. He is the second man that I have ever seen and I feel sure that he is a good man."

6

FREDINAND PASSES THE TEST

Prospero pretended to be very angry. "Be quiet," he ordered her. "You're wasting your pity on a spy. You think that he is a fine figure of a man because you've seen only Caliban. I tell you that there are thousands of men far finer than he is."

"There may be," Miranda answered him quietly, "but I have no wish to see a finer man."

"Come with me. Come on. You have no power to disobey me," Prospero said to Ferdinand.

"Indeed I have not," the prince had to admit. He followed Prospero but he kept looking back all the time at Miranda. He was filled with wonder. "Is this a dream?" he asked himself. "Is it a beautiful, beautiful dream? O, I can bear anything—this man's harsh words, my own strange weakness, anything,—if only I can see this lovely maiden once a day!"

Prospero found some hard tasks for Ferdinand to perform.

"Pile up these logs of wood," he commanded him harshly. Ferdinand obeyed but he soon grew tired, for he was not used to such hard work. Miranda found him sitting exhausted by the logs.

"Don't work so hard," she begged him. "My father is at his books. He won't come out of his study for three hours at least. Have a rest."

Miranda thought that her father was in his study but he was not. Invisible to them, he was standing nearby and listening to all they said. He was delighted to find that the two were so much in love.

"I can't take any rest till I've finished my task," Ferdinand told Miranda.

"If you will sit down. I'll carry your logs for you," Miranda told him. Ferdinand refused to let her do this. They began to talk and soon Ferdinand forgot all about finishing his task.

"What is your name?" Ferdinand asked her.

"Miranda," she answered, telling him her name although her father had commanded her not to do so. Prospero had to smile at this. The young prince began to praise her beauty which he called "divine". "I do not know," she replied simply, "for I don't remember any other woman's face. Except for my father's, yours is the only man's face that I have seen. But I like it and I like you." Miranda smiled and shook her head. "I'm afraid I am talking too freely to you and forgetting my father's commands." Little did she know that her father was smiling with delight at her forgetfulness!

In a fine speech, Ferdinand told her that one day he would be King of Naples and she should be his queen. This made Miranda weep for joy. She answered him very simply, "I am your wife if you will marry me."

Prospero had heard enough. He was now sure that they loved each other truly. He therefore made himself visible and said, with the kindest of smiles, "I have overheard all. Ferdinand, I have treated you harshly, I admit, but I'll make up for it by giving you my daughter. I merely wanted to test the strength of your love. You have shown that your love is true and strong. Take my daughter as a gift which your love has bought. She is a gift beyond all price." Prospero kissed Miranda, saying, "I must leave you now, for I have work to do elsewhere. Sit down and talk till I come back." Miranda and Ferdinand were happy to obey.

7

ARIEL DOES HIS WORK WELL

Prospero called Ariel to him. "Well, my brave spirit, what news of my brother and the King of Naples?" he asked him.

Ariel laughed. "I left them almost out of their sense," he said "They were half-dead with hunger and weariness. I set a most delicious feast in front of

them. Then, just as they were going to eat it, I flew down in the form of a winged monster. The feast disappeared from their sight but I remained and I spoke to them. I reminded them of their evil treatment of you and told them that they were being punished for it. You should have seen their faces! They were filled with remorse at their wicked deeds. They were so miserable that I had to pity them."

"If you pity them, Ariel, then I, as a human being like themselves, ought to pity them all the more. Bring them here at once, my pretty Ariel."

Ariel flew off obediently. With wild music, Ariel drew the repentant men to Prospero's cave. With them came kind Gonzalo who, twelve years before, had helped Prospero in his distress.

At first the three men did not recognise Prospero in his magician's robe and with his long white beard, but when Prospero thanked Gonzalo for saving his life and that of his daughter, they all knew who he was. Antonio instantly begged Prospero's forgiveness and so did the King of Naples. Prospero readily forgave them. They promised to give him back his dukedom. To the King of Naples, Prospero said, "I have something to give you too." So saying, he opened a door and showed them Ferdinand who was playing chess with Miranda.

Great was the joy of father and son to find each other alive and well. Miranda was filled with wonder. "What noble creature these are!" she exclaimed. "It must surely be a beautiful world that has such fine people in it."

The King of Naples was astonished at the beauty and charm of Miranda. Like Ferdinand, he took her for a goddess. "I shall be happy to be another father to you," he told Miranda, "but, O, how strangely will it sound that I must beg my daughter to forgive me!"

8

ALL ARE HAPPY

"Let us all forgive and forget," said Prospero. "Our troubles are all over now. All this has happened as God willed. God willed that I should be driven from Milan and brought to this island. On this island Miranda and Ferdinand met and fell in love. Let us praise almighty God!"

Hearing this, Antonio wept for shame. Kind old Gonzalo wept too, but he was weeping with joy at the happiness of the two lovers. "God bless them!" he said.

Prospero then assured his guests that their ship and all the crew were safe. They were all going to leave for Naples the next morning. "In the meantime," said Prospero, "I offer you the hospitality of my cave." He called for Caliban to prepare a meal and to set the cave in order. Great was the astonishment of his guests at being waited on by such an ugly monster!

Before he left the island, Prospero buried his books on magic deep in the earth, and his magic wand as well. He would never more use his magic power. Why should he? He had obtained all that he wished for. He had brought his brother and the King of Naples to repentance. He had received his dukedom back. Above all, Miranda was going to marry Ferdinand, the King of Naples's heir and the man she loved.

Prospero now turned to Ariel and gave him his freedom. "My pretty Ariel," he said sadly, "I shall miss you very much. But, go! You are now free." Ariel was filled with delight.

He flew away, singing this Pretty song:

"Where the bee sucks, there suck I.
In a cowslip's bell I lie;
There I couch when owls do cry.
On the bat's back I do fly
After summer merrily.
Merrily, merrily shall I live now
Under the blossom that hangs on the bough."

MACBETH

The People in the Story

Macbeth	:	A nobleman and a relative of Duncan.
Duncan	:	The King of Scotland.
Lord of Cawdor	:	A nobleman rebelling against Duncan.
Banquo	:	A general fighting with Macbeth.
Lady Macbeth	:	Macbeth's wife.
Malcolm	:	Duncan's elder son.
Fleance	:	Banquo's son.
Macduff	:	The chief of the nobles.

MACBETH

1

MACBETH'S RETURN FROM BATTLE

Macbeth, lord of *Glamis*, was a Scottish nobleman and a relative of *Duncan, King of Scotland*. He was a skilful and brave leader in battle. For this reason, he was held in high honour by the King, the nobles, and the people.

King Duncan sent Macbeth with a large army to fight against the lord of *Cawdor* who had risen in rebellion against him. Macbeth was able to defeat the rebel army after a bloody battle. He was returning from the battlefield when a strange thing happened. He and another general, *Banquo* by name, were crossing a wild and desolate heath when suddenly three witches appeared before them. They were dreadful to see. Macbeth, however, was not afraid.

"Who are you? You look like women but you have beards like men. Tell us who you are and what you want," said Macbeth.

The witches did not answer his question. The first of them cried out,

"All hail, Macbeth! All hail to the Lord of Glamis!"

The second cried out, "All hail to the Lord of Cawdor!"

The third cried out, "All hail to Macbeth who will soon be King!"

The dreadful creatures turned to Banquo. The first of them said, "All hail to Banquo! Lesser than Macbeth and greater!"

The second witch cried out, "Not so happy, yet much happier!"

The third said, "You will not be king but your descendants will be king."

The witches then vanished as suddenly as they had appeared.

2

MACBETH BECOMES AMBITIOUS

Macbeth and Banquo were much astonished by all this. They were talking about the strange happening when two nobles came up to them. "The king," they told Macbeth and Banquo, "has sent us to congratulate you on your great victory. He has taken the title from the Lord of Cawdor and now gives it to Macbeth as a sign of his pleasure."

Macbeth was amazed. The witches' prophecy had come true, and so soon! They had called him "Lord of Cawdor" and now indeed he was. His thoughts flew to their second prophecy: they had said that he would soon be king. Would that also come true? He turned to Banquo.

"Now you can hope that your descendants will become kings," he told him.

In his mind was the thought, "Now I can hope to become king soon."

"I don't believe them," Banquo said. "They are evil and they want to tempt us to do evil. You shouldn't believe them."

Macbeth, however, did believe them and rejoiced. Why should he not become king? Duncan was old and sick. Duncan was a weak ruler and the land needed a strong one. It needed Macbeth! So ran Macbeth's thoughts.

3

LADY MACBETH IS ALSO AMBITIOUS

The king wished to show how much he honoured Macbeth, so, according to the custom of that time, he promised to pay a visit to Macbeth's castle. Macbeth at once left the palace to tell his wife of the coming visit. He sent a messenger ahead of him with a letter for *Lady Macbeth*. In the letter he told his wife of the prophecies of the three witches. The first, he said, had come true already. Would the second come true too?

Lady Macbeth looked very thoughtful after reading the letter. She was an ambitious woman and she was determined to do all she could to make her husband king. King Duncan was the obstacle in their path. Well, they must get rid of him. She would urge her husband to kill him. This would be hard, for Macbeth was not as determined and as merciless by nature as she was. He was, she knew, "too full of the milk of human kindness". She therefore decided to urge him on to murder.

The king was coming to their castle. This was their opportunity. They would kill him on the night of his arrival. Who would suspect Macbeth? His loyalty towards the king was praised by all. Nobody would suspect him.

As soon as Macbeth arrived, she told him all that was in her mind. She saw that he, too, was eager to get rid of Duncan but he was afraid to kill him.

4

MACBETH STRUGGLES WITH TEMPTATION

King Duncan arrived and was delighted with the warm welcome he received. He praised the castle and its beautiful gardens. "Here the air is sweet," he told his host. "Here all is calm and quiet. I can rest in peace under your roof." As a sign of his pleasure, he sent a magnificent diamond to Lady Macbeth. The old king went to bed with his mind filled with peaceful thoughts.

Macbeth, on the other hand, was tormented by fears and doubts. "How can I kill the king?" he asked himself. "He is my cousin and a man cannot murder his kinsman. Besides this, Duncan is my guest, and a host ought to protect his guest." However, the temptation to kill the king was strong. "If I kill him, I shall be king. The witches promised that I should be...." So ran his wicked thoughts.

Macbeth struggled hard against this temptation. For a moment he won. "I cannot kill the king," he told Lady Macbeth. "He has given me high honours and I am grateful to him. The people praise me for my loyalty and bravery and I value their praise. I will be satisfied with what I have."

Lady Macbeth turned on him angrily. She called him a coward. "You haven't the courage to take what you most desire," she told him. "Be a man!" Then she tempted him further by describing how easy it would be to kill Duncan. Nobody would suspect Macbeth.

5

THE DEED IS DONE

Macbeth listened to his wife. He agreed that the king must be killed in his sleep. As part of their plan, they drugged the wine of the two guards who slept in the king's room. Then, when everyone was asleep and the castle silent, Lady Macbeth stole in the king's room.

The king and his guards were asleep. Lady Macbeth raised her dagger to strike. But then, in the moonlight, she saw his face. It reminded her of that of her dead father. Her hand fell to her side. She could not kill Duncan. She stole away as silently as she had come. She handed the dagger to Macbeth and told him to go and kill the king.

Macbeth took the dagger. In the darkness he made his way to Duncan's room. As he drew near it, a terrible vision appeared before him. He saw a dagger that was dripping blood and pointing towards his heart. He put out his hand to grasp it, but immediately it disappeared. With a great effort, Macbeth shook off his fear and tiptoed into the king's room. He struck at Duncan's heart and, in a single stroke, killed the old king.

Macbeth crept to the door. Suddenly he stopped. One of the guards had laughed in his sleep. The other cried out "Murder!". Both guards awoke and looked around them sleepily. Then both feel asleep again.

6

MACBETH FEELS REMORSE

Lady Macbeth was waiting anxiously for her husband to return. She was listening to every sound. When she heard the guards cry out, she thought that Macbeth had failed. Eventually, however, Macbeth came back and told her hoarsely that the deed was done. He walked wildly up and down. A voice seemed to be crying continuously in his ear: "Sleep no more! Macbeth has murdered sleep, innocent sleep, the nurse of life. Glamis has murdered sleep and therefore Cawdor shall sleep no more. Macbeth shall sleep no more."

Lady Macbeth scolded him for his weakness. "Have you lost your senses?" she asked him angrily. "Why have you brought the dagger back? Take it and lay it at the side of the guards. Stain their clothes with blood."

But Macbeth refused to go back into the room where Duncan lay dead. Lady Macbeth had to go herself. She lay the dagger beside the sleeping guards and smeared them with Duncan's blood. When she returned, she found Macbeth gazing at his hands in horror. "Will all the water in the ocean be enough to wash these hands clean?" he asked in terror. "No. This blood will turn the entire ocean red," he told his wife, for he was almost mad with fear and remorse.

7

THE SECOND PROPHECY IS FULFILLED

Suddenly in the silence of the night, a knocking was heard. Somebody was knocking at the castle gate. Macbeth trembled like a leaf at the sudden sound. His guilty conscience had turned him into a coward. He wished that the knocking were able to awaken the dead king. He was filled with remorse at what he had done. Then Lady Macbeth whispered to him urgently, "Go and wash your hands. Put on your nightgown. Quick! Nobody must think that we haven't been to bed. Hurry!"

Outside a storm was raging. To Macbeth it seemed that the heavens were proclaiming his bloody deed. The knocking at the gate grew louder. The sleepy porter went to open the gate.

Two of King Duncan's noble attendants had arrived early in order to attend the king. They went to Duncan's room and found him dead. Instantly, the castle was filled with fear and confusion. When they told Macbeth of the murder, he showed great anger. In pretended fury, he killed Duncan's two guards. In this way, he hoped to show his love and loyalty to the king. Duncan's sons, who were also in the castle, were not deceived. They did not suspect the guards, for what had they to gain from the murder of the king? They feared for their own safety. *Malcolm*, the elder son, fled at once to England while his brother fled to Ireland. In their absence, Macbeth was proclaimed Duncan's heir and King of Scotland. The witches' second prophecy was fulfilled!

8

"YOUR DESCENDANTS WILL BE KINGS"

Macbeth had obtained what he wanted. He was now King of Scotland. But he did not feel safe on his throne. His guilty conscience troubled him and he mistrusted everyone. Especially did he mistrust and fear Banquo. He remembered what the witches had promised Banquo: "You will not be king, Banquo, but your descendants will be kings." Macbeth and his wife now asked themselves if they had killed Duncan only to benefit Banquo's family. Besides this, Banquo knew too much. He had heard what the witches had said to Macbeth. He knew that Macbeth had a motive for the murder. Banquo was dangerous. He must die and so must his son.

Macbeth and his wife planned to get rid of Banquo and his son *Fleance*. They invited the chief nobles to a banquet at which Banquo was the guest of honour. Macbeth then hired two murderers to attack and kill Banquo and Fleance as they were riding to the castle. The murderers were able to kill Banquo but Fleance escaped. He fled to England. Long afterwards, a line of kings descended from Fleance ruled Scotland. In this way, the witches' prophecy about Banquo also came true.

BANQUO'S GHOST

The noble guests arrived for the banquet and were received most courteously by their new King and Queen. It was not long before the absence of Banquo was noticed. "I wonder what has happened to him," said Macbeth to his guests. "I hope that he hasn't had an accident. I wish he were here."

As soon as he said this, the ghost of Banquo appeared in the

chair reserved for him. Macbeth gazed at it in horror. "Do not shake your bloody hair at me! You can't say that I did it," he whispered hoarsely. Nobody else saw the ghost and everybody wondered what was the matter with their host. Lady Macbeth tried to explain, "My lord is often like this. It is nothing. Take no notice. He will soon be well." She took her husband aside and whispered to him, "Be a man and hide your fear. If you don't, they'll suspect us. What's the matter with you? You're only looking at a chair!"

At that moment, the ghost disappeared and Macbeth felt brave again. He chattered with his guests and drank to the health of all of them. He drank to the health of his "dear friend" Banquo. "I wish he were here," he said again. Immediately the ghost of Banquo re-appeared. Macbeth shook with terror. "Away, horrible shadow!" he screamed. "Away, out of my sight! Let the earth cover you up!" He was quite out of his mind.

The banquet broke up in confusion. Lady Macbeth again tried to explain that her husband often had fits of this kind. But she read suspicion on many faces and hurried the guests away. The nobles had seen enough to make them suspect Macbeth. *Macduff*, the chief of the nobles, had not come to the banquet, for he suspected treachery. Macbeth now had many enemies. He became merciless and was prepared to get rid of anyone who opposed him. He was full of fears for the future and he decided to go and consult the three witches. They had prophesied truly before. He would ask them to prophesy again for he wanted to know the worst.

10

MACBETH CONSULTS THE WITCHES AGAIN

Macbeth found the witches on that wild and lonely heath where he had first met them. They were expecting him and were preparing evil spells to call spirits from the dead. These spirits would reveal the future. In a large kettle they were boiling a horrid mixture. This was made up of toads, bats, snakes, the tooth of a wolf, the belly of a shark, the gall of a goat, the dried flesh of a witch and the finger of a dead child. From time to time, they poured in the blood of a monkey and that of a sow that had eaten its young.

"Tell me what is going to

happen," Macbeth asked them. In answer, they called for three ghosts to appear. The first had the form of a soldier's head, with a helmet on it. This ghost addressed Macbeth in a solemn tone, saying:

"Macbeth! Macbeth! Macbeth! Beware Macduff! Beware the *Lord of Fife*!" Then it vanished.

With the noise of thunder, the second ghost appeared in the form of the bloody head of a child. "Be bloody, bold and resolute," it urged Macbeth. "No man who

is born of a woman can ever harm you." "Then," thought Macbeth, "Macduff cannot harm me. All the same, I shall feel safer when he is dead." He instantly made up his mind that Macduff must be killed.

The third ghost now made its appearance. This was in the form of a child wearing a crown on its head and carrying a tree in its hand. "Fear nothing!" it said. "You have no need to fear. You will never be defeated until *Birnam Wood* comes to *Dunsinane Hill*." Then it too vanished beneath the earth.

Macbeth now felt happier. He believed the third ghost. There was no need to fear his enemies, for how could a forest uproot itself and march? There was, however, one question which he had to ask: "Will Banquo's descen-dants reign in Scotland?" The witches warned him not to ask that question but Macbeth insisted. Then, to the sound of music, eight shadows passed before him, the shadows of eight kings. Last of all came Banquo, all covered in blood. He was holding a looking-glass in his hand. In it, Macbeth saw more of Banquo's descendants' wearing the Scottish crown. He gazed at them in despair. "No more! I'll see no more!" he shouted wildly to the witches. At this, the three foul creatures vanished. From that time, the thoughts of Macbeth were bloody and devilish.

11

"NOT SO HAPPY"

Soon after this, Macbeth heard that Macduff had fled to England. This news made him wild with anger. Macduff, his chief enemy, was now out of his reach. He was with Malcolm and Fleance and they were gathering an army to attack Macbeth. Macbeth then took a fearful revenge. He attacked Macduff's castle, killed his wife and children and everyone he found there. This evil deed did Macbeth great harm. Many nobles turned

against him and went to join Malcolm who was now advancing from England with a strong army.

Macbeth was now desperate. His nobles hated him. There was not a single one of them who honoured him. All of them looked on him as a murderer. Macbeth wished that he were dead, as Duncan was. He envied the king his peaceful sleep. Neither steel nor poison, hatred at home or enemies abroad, could hurt the dead king or disturb his peaceful sleep.

Lady Macbeth was also tormented by the evil she had done.

She had urged her husband to commit the first crime. From that first crime, how many others had followed! Her guilt weighed heavily on her conscience. Like her husband, she had lost all peace of mind and hope of happiness. In this way, the witches' prophecy to Banquo was fulfilled. They had called him, "Lesser than Macbeth and greater. Not so happy and yet much happier." How true that was!

As Macbeth grew more merciless, Lady Macbeth blamed herself more and more. She could not sleep at night or, if she did sleep, she would walk in her sleep. Night after night, her attendants would see her trying to wash her hands and saying sadly, "All the perfumes in Arabia will not sweeten this little hand!" Her doctor could do nothing to help her. "I have no medicine for an illness like hers," he said. "The cause of it is a guilty conscience and only God can help her."

Unable to bear her tormented life any longer, Lady Macbeth killed herself.

12

MACBETH'S AGONY

After Lady Macbeth's death, Macbeth was left without a single friend. He longed for death. When he heard that Malcolm was approaching with a large army, some of his old courage came back to him. He found few men ready to fight for him. All the same, he was determined to resist as long as he could and to die "with armour on his back". He shut himself up in his castle at Dunsinane. There he comforted himself with the prophecies of the three witches. Had they not said that he could not be harmed by any man born of a woman? Had they not promised that he would never be defeated until Birnam Wood marched to Dunsinane Hill? And of course that was impos-sible. So Macbeth believed but he was soon proved wrong. A messenger came running to him. He was deadly pale and shaking with such fear that he was almost unable to speak. "Birnam Wood is marching towards Dunsinane Hill!" he gasped.

"Liar!" shouted Macbeth. "If you are lying, I'll hang you from the nearest tree. If you are speaking the truth, you can do the same to me. I don't care." His courage left him for he realised how the witches had betrayed him. "I begin to be weary of the sun," he said. "I wish my life were at the end." Then he shouted, "To arms! March out! There's no escape for us. Let us die fighting in the open!"

13

HOW BIRNAM WOOD CAME TO DUNSINANE HILL

Birnam Wood was not marching to Dunsinane. What had happened was this: When Malcolm had reached the forest, he had ordered each soldier to cut a branch from a tree and to carry it in front of him. In this way it would be hard for Macbeth to find out the real numbers of his enemies. Malcolm hoped that he could deceive Macbeth and make him think his army was smaller than it really was. Thus Macbeth would be tempted to leave his castle and to fight in open country where Malcolm would have the advantage.

A bloody battle began. Macbeth fought with all his former strength and courage. His hope was in the witches' prophecy: "You can never be harmed by any man born of a woman." His men supported him weakly, for they had no faith in their leader nor in his cause. Macbeth killed all who came against him. At last he found himself face to face with Macduff who had been

looking for him in the thick of the battle. Macduff, who was burning for revenge, rushed at him, shouting, "Murderer! Hell-hound! Villain!"

"Get back!" Macbeth shouted to him, "I've already killed too many of your family."

Macduff was determined to kill Macbeth and a fierce struggle began. Blow answered blow till both men were exhausted. There was a brief pause while each was recovering his strength. Then Macbeth cried out, "You're wasting your strength, Macduff. I have a charmed life. No man born of a woman can ever harm me."

Macduff laughed. "I was not born of a woman," he cried. "I was taken from my mother's womb before the due time."

Macbeth knew that the witches had deceived him and he cursed them. His courage left him. "I will not fight against you," he told Macduff.

"Live then," Macduff mocked him. "We'll put you in a cage and show you at fairs, with the notice: HERE YOU MAY SEE THE TYRANT.

"Never!" shouted Macbeth. "I will never live to kiss the ground at Malcolm's feet and to be cursed by the people." Then he threw aside his shield and attacked Macduff furiously. "Come on! And a curse be on the one who first cries 'Enough'!"

Macduff proved to be the stronger. He killed Macbeth and showed his head to Malcolm and his army. The witches' prophecy—"Beware Macduff!" had come true!"

Thus ended the life of Macbeth, a brave and noble soldier whose ambition had destroyed him.

A MID-SUMMER NIGHT'S DREAM

The People in the Story

Egeus	:	An Athenian nobleman.
Duke Theseus	:	Duke of Athens.
Hermia	:	Daughter of Egeus.
Helena	:	Hermia's friend who loved Demetrius.
Demetrius	:	The man chosen by Egeus to be Hermia's husband.
Lysander	:	Hermia's true lover.
Oberon	:	King of the fairies in Fairyland.
Titania	:	Queen of the fairies in Fairyland.
Puck	:	The merriest and most mischievous of Oberon's fairies.
Bottom	:	A simple, stupid country fellow.
Pease-blossom **Cobweb** **Moth** **Mustard-seed**	}	Titania's fairies

A MIDSUMMER NIGHT'S DREAM

1

THE PROBLEM

Long ago, it was the custom in *Athens* for a father to choose the husband for his daughter. There was also a cruel law which said that a daughter who refused to marry the man of her father's choice could be put to death. Luckily, this law was seldom or never put into force.

One day, an Athenian nobleman, *Egeus* by name, came before *Duke Theseus* with a complaint about his daughter. His daughter *Hermia* had refused to marry *Demetrius,* the man he had chosen for her husband. Hermia was in love with *Lysander* and said that she would marry no one but him. As for Lysander, he had been so bold as to say that his love for Hermia gave him the right to marry her!

Hermia defended herself by saying that she did not like Demetrius, the man of her father's choice. Demetrius, so she told the Duke, had won the heart of her dear

friend *Helena*. Helena was very much in love with him and he ought to marry her.

Duke Theseus sympathised with Hermia and Lysander, for he himself was young enough to know the power of love. However, he had to show respect for the law and for old Egeus. Accordingly, he gave Hermia four days in which to consider the matter. If, after four days, she would not obey her father, then she must die!

2

LYSANDER'S PLAN

When Hermia heard this harsh sentence, she hurried to Lysander to tell him all. Then Lysander remembered that he had a wealthy aunt, a childless widow, who lived some twenty miles outside Athens, beyond the reach of the Athenian laws. He suggested that they should flee to his aunt's home and there they would get married.

"Steal away from your father's house this very night," he urged his Hermia. "I'll be waiting for you in the wood just outside the city. You know the place well. It's where we used to play as children, the place where we went for such delightful walks with Helena in the merry month of May."

Hermia gladly agreed to do so. Helena, her bosom-friend,

then joined the lovers and they told her of their plan, for they trusted her entirely. But Helena, out of love for Demetrius, told him of their plan. She knew that Demetrius would follow Hermia and so she would have the chance of following Demetrius. Poor, foolish Helena! She had betrayed her friend in order to have the pleasure of following the man who no longer loved her. She was quite madly in love with Demetrius.

3

TROUBLE IN FAIRYLAND

The wood where the lovers were going to meet was the favourite haunt of the fairies. It was here that they used to have their midnight revels. Lately, however, there had been no revelry. The wood had become a sad and silent place. The reason for this was a quarrel between the fairy king *Oberon* and his queen *Titania*. Titania had stolen a little boy from his nurse and she loved the boy so much that she refused to left Oberon have him. Now, whenever Oberon and Titania met, there was such quarrelling that their attendant fairies were afraid and ran away to hide in seed-pods.

On the night when the lovers were going to meet, Titania and Oberon met by chance.

"I'll-met by moon-light, proud Titania!" cried the fairy king.

"What! Is it you, jealous Oberon?" Titania answered him. She called to her fairies, "Let's go away. I'll have nothing to do with Oberon."

"Wait, foolish fairy!" Oberon commanded. "I am your master and you must listen to me. Give me that little boy. I've told you how much I want him as my page."

"I will not. I would not let you have him even if you offered me the whole of your kingdom," Titania replied, turning away angrily and proudly.

"Well, go your way," said Oberon. "Before morning you will be sorry for this," he threatened.

4

OBERON'S PLAN

Oberon called *Puck* who was the merriest and the most mischievous of his fairies. Puck delighted in all kinds of mischief. In the village nearby, they knew him well. It was Puck who turned the milk sour in the dairy. It was Puck who stole the cream. It was Puck who pulled the stool from under a good old dame when she was sitting down to tell a sad and sorrowful tale. This made the old women round her laugh till their sides ached and swear that they had never had such a good laugh for ages.

"Puck," said Oberon to this merry wanderer of the night, "fetch me that flower which maidens call ëLove in Idleness'. The juice of that little purple flower, put on the eyelids of those who sleep, will make them, when they awake, fall madly in love with the first living thing that they see. I will drop some of this juice on the eyelids of my Titania while she is sleeping. Then, when she wakes, she will fall in love with the first living being that she sees. This may be a lion, a bear, a monkey or even an ape! And I shall not remove this charm until she has promised to give me that boy as my page."

Puck was delightful with this errand and at once flew off in search of the magic flower.

5

OBERON TRIES TO HELP HERMIA

While Oberon was waiting for Puck to return, he saw Demetrius and Helena enter the wood. Invisible to them, he watched and overheard their conversation.

"Why are you following me?" Demetrius was asking Helena in anger. "I've told you that I no longer love you. It's Hermia that I love, and I'm going to marry her. Go away, I tell you. Go!"

Helena answered him gently, reminding him that not so long ago he had said that he loved her and that he always would. "You have changed but I have not," she told him sadly "My love for you will never change. I must follow you, whether you like it or not."

Demetrius did not answer her but plunged into some thorny bushes where, he hoped, Helena would not be able to follow him. But she struggled after him all the same.

Oberon, who was the friend of all true lovers, pitied her with all his heart. And so, when Puck came back with that little purple flower, he said to him.

"Take a part of this flower...I've just seen a lovely lady from Athens who is in love with a most cruel youth. Squeeze some juice on his eyelids when he is asleep. But be sure to do it when she is nearby. She must be the first person that he sees when he wakes up, so that he will fall in love with her. You will know the man by the Athenian garments he has on."

6
OBERON PUTS A SPELL ON TITANIA

Away flew Puck on this new errand. Oberon, who had kept a part of the magic flower, went to look for Titania. He found her on a bank where many sweet-smelling flowers were growing. There she always slept some part of the night. Her bed-cover was the skin of a snake which was just wide enough to wrap a fairy in. Under a roof of climbing roses, she was giving her fairies their tasks for the night.

"Some of you must go and kill the worms that are eating the rosebuds. Some of you must make war on the bats. I need their leather wings to make coats for my small fairies. Some of you must keep the hooting owl away. But, first of all, you must sing me to sleep."

When Titania was asleep, Oberon softly drew near her. He dropped some of the love-juice on her eyelids, saying,

"What thou seest when thou dost wake

Do it for thy true love take."

When he had done this, he flew away.

7

PUCK MAKES A MISTAKE

In the meantime, what was happening to Hermia and Lysander?

Hermia had stolen from her father's house and had found Lysander waiting for her in the wood. They had walked on and on till they were both tired out. Hermia could go no farther and lay down on a soft green bank. Lysander lay down a little farther off. Worn out with wandering, they were soon fast asleep.

Here Puck came upon them. Lysander was also wearing Athenian clothes, and thinking he was the man Oberon meant, he dropped some of the love-juice on Lysander's eyelids. Then away he flew. The mistake would not have mattered if Lysander had seen Hermia when he awoke. But, by chance, it was Helena that he saw first!

Helena had followed Demetrius as far as she had been able to, but when her strength failed her, she could follow him no farther. She wandered on, sad and lonely, till she came across

Lysander lying fast asleep on the ground. She touched him gently, saying, "Good Lysander, if you are alive, wake up!"

Lysander opened his eyes. The love-juice at once did its work and he felt that he was madly in love with Helena. He began to speak to her in a lover-like manner. "I would run through fire for your sweet sake," he told her. When she reminded him of his love for Hermia, he said, "Hermia! Her beauty is nothing compared with yours. Compared with you, she is like a raven beside a dove."

Helena knew that Lysander had promised to marry Hermia whom he deeply loved. She was therefore very angry, for she thought that he was making a fool of her. "Oh," she exclaimed, "why was I born to be mocked at by everybody? Isn't it enough that I can never get a kind word from Demetrius? Must you, sir, in this cruel manner, pretend to love me? I thought, Lysander, that you were too kind to tease a poor lady so!"

Helena ran away in anger. Lysander ran after her. Poor Hermia was left behind, still fast asleep.

8
RESULTS OF TWO MISTAKES

When Hermia awoke and saw that she was alone, she was very frightened. Where was Lysander? She wandered about the wood, calling, "Lysander! Lysander!"

but Lysander did not answer.

In the meantime, Demetrius, who had been looking for Hermia in vain, had lain down to sleep. Oberon found him and recognised him as the cruel lover. He at once dropped some of the magic juice on Demetrius's eyelids. When Demetrius awoke, the first person that he saw was Helena. She was running by, pursued by Lysander. Instantly Demetrius felt that he loved Helena madly. Like Lysander, he began to speak to her in the tender words of a lover. Lysander burst upon them, with Hermia close behind him. It was now Hermia's turn to pursue her lover!

Lysander and Demetrius were now rivals for the love of Helena just as before they had been rivals for the love of Hermia. Poor Helena thought that both of them were making fun of her. Angrily she reproached them thus:

"If you were men, as men you are in show.
You would not use a gentle lady so;
To vow and swear and super-praise my parts,
When, I am sure, you hate me in your hearts."

9

HERMIA AND HELENA QUARREL

Hermia was angry and astonished. Lysander and Demetrius had both loved her. Suddenly both had transferred their love to Helena! Hermia and Helena, who had been bosom-friends, now became bitter enemies!

Helena turned to Hermia. "Unkind Hermia," she said, "it's all your fault. You've told the men to make a fool of me. And you're joining with them to laugh at your poor friend. Oh, Hermia, have you forgotten our life-long friendship? Haven't we always worked and played together? Haven't we embroi-dered together. Don't you remember how we used to sit on the same cushion, singing the same song, embroidering the same flower? We've grown up together like a double cherry. Hermia, it's so unfriendly of you; it's very unkind and unmaidenly to join with men in laughing at me!"

Hermia turned on Helena. "I'm not laughing at you. It's you who are laughing at me, you false friend, you witch!"

Hermia and Helena grew more and more angry and began to call each other most unladylike names. While they were quarrelling, Lysander and Demetrius went off to fight a duel for love of Helena.

10

OBERON'S PLAN TO RIGHT A WRONG

Unseen by the lovers, Oberon and Puck had been listening to their quarrelling. "This is your carelessness, Puck," said Oberon. "Or did you do it on purpose?"

"Believe me, *King of Shadows,* it was a mistake," Puck answered him. Didn't you tell me that I should know the man by the Athenian garments he had on?" Puck laughed merrily "I can't say that I'm sorry that this has happened," he told Oberon. "It's good fun to watch."

Oberon looked stern. "The joke has gone too far, Puck. Go and fill the night with a thick fog. Lead these quarrelsome lovers far away from each other. Lead them on till they are weary and can go no farther. Then when they fall down exhausted, send them to sleep. While Lysander is sleeping, drop a little of the juice from this different flower on his eyelids. When he awakes, he'll forget his new love for Helena and remember only his old love for Hermia. That will make both ladies happy. They'll begin to think that they've had a strange dream. They'll become friends again. Go and do this at once, Puck, I must go and see what kind of lover my Titania has found."

11

TITANIA IN LOVE WITH BOTTOM

Titania was asleep in her fragrant bower. Not far away there was, by chance, a simple, stupid country fellow named *Bottom* who had lost his way in the wood. Overcome by weariness, he had fallen asleep. Oberon went up to him. He put an ass's head over Bottom's head, and it fitted him perfectly. When he awoke, he began to wander about and, in his wanderings, he reached

Titania's bower.

"Oh, what angel do I see?" asked the fairy queen, opening her eyes and feeling the influence of the love-juice. "Are you as wise as you are beautiful?" she asked tenderly.

"Mistress, if only I had wit enough to find my way out of this wood, I'd think I was wise enough," said Bottom with a loud "Hee-Haw".

"Out of this wood do not desire to go. I love you. Stay with me. You shall have all my fairies to wait on you."

Titania then called four of her fairies, *Pease-blossom, Cobweb, Moth* and *Mustard-seed*. "Wait on this sweet gentleman," she told them. "Feed him with grapes and apricots. Steal the honey-bags from the bees for him to eat." Tenderly she said to the country fellow with the ass's head, "Come and sit beside me. Let me play with your pretty hairy cheeks, my beautiful ass! Let me kiss your lovely long ears, my gentle joy!"

12

BOTTOM IS WELL LOOKED AFTER

"Where's Pease-blossom?" asked the ass-headed Bottom.

"Here, sir," answered little Pease-blossom.

"Scratch my head. It itches. Where's Cobweb?"

"Here, sir," said Cobweb.

"Good, Mr. Cobweb, please kill that red bee on the top of that bush over there. And bring me its honey-bag. Take care it doesn't break. You'll be in a fine mess if it does. Where's Mustard-seed?"

"Here, sir,"

"Good Mr. Mustard-seed, help Mr. Pease-blossom to scratch. I must go to the barber's, Mr. Mustard-seed, for I seem to have a lot of hair on my face."

"My sweet love," said Titania, "what would you like to eat?"

"A handful of dried peas," Bottom told her for, with his ass's head, he had also an ass's taste. "But I'd like to have a sleep."

"Sleep then, and I'll hold you in my arms. Ah, how I love you! How madly I love you!"

Titania put a crown of flowers on his ass's head and he fell asleep in the arms of the fairy queen.

13

OBERON OBTAINS WHAT HE WANTS

Just then, Oberon came upon them.

"Aren't you ashamed, Titania?" Oberon asked his queen. He laughed loud and long at her folly. Titania was indeed ashamed. When Oberon asked her again for

the boy, she agreed to let him have him, for she dared not refuse.

Oberon took pity on her. He dropped some of the juice from a different flower on to her eyelids and so released her from the magic spell. Titania was astonished at her own folly. She now said that she hated the sight of that ugly, hairy monster. Oberon removed the ass's head and left him to sleep with his own fool's head on his shoulders.

Oberon and Titania were now friends again. He told her the story of the enchanted lovers and she went with him to see the end of their adventures.

14

THE LOVERS PROPERLY MATCHED

The fairy king and queen found the lovers sleeping, not far from each other, on a grassy back. Puck had brought them all to the same spot and had removed the love-juice from Lysander's eyes.

Hermia woke first and found Lysander near her. She gazed at him in astonishment, wondering over his strange behaviour. He

opened his eyes and smiled joyfully at seeing her. He now loved her as he had done before. They began to talk over the strange things that had happened and concluded that they had been dreaming.

Helena and Demetrius awoke a little later. Helena's bad temper had gone and she listened joyfully to Demetrius's loving words, for they seemed to her quite true.

The ladies were close friends again and so were the men. All unkind words and deeds were forgiven and forgotten. What had happened in the night seemed unreal, like something in a dream. The lovers began to think what they should do next. Demetrius, they agreed, should return to Athens. He should tell Egeus that he was going to marry Helena whom he dearly loved. He would also beg Egeus to let Hermia marry Lysander.

15

A HAPPY ENDING

Demetrius was just starting out for Athens when Duke Theseus and his queen came upon them. They were out hunting with a large company, among whom was old Egeus. Duke Theseus wanted to know what they were all doing in the wood so early in the morning. Lysander confessed that he and Hermia had stolen away in order to escape the cruel law. Demetrius explained that he no longer wanted to marry Hermia but he preferred Helena. Duke Theseus thought that this was a happy end to the story. Egeus agreed to the marriage of Hermia and Lysander.

Oberon and Titania, invisible as they were, had watched and listened to all this. They were delighted with the happy end and decided to celebrate it with feasting and revelry. As a result, there was great joy not only in Athens but also in fairyland for the wedding of Lysander and Hermia, Demetrius and Helena.

You may think that this story is too strange to be believed. If you do, think of it as a dream, a beautiful midsummer night's dream!

JULIUS CAESAR

The People in the Story

Pompry	:	A very powerful general in Rome.
Julius Caesar	:	The most powerful general in Rome.
Mark Antony	:	Julius Caesar's chief officer.
Brutus	:	Julius Caesar's most trusted friend.
Cassius	:	A senator and a friend of Brutus.
Casca	:	Friend of Cassius.
Portia	:	Wife of Brutus.
Calpurnia	:	Wife of Caesar.
Decius	:	One of the conspirators against Julius Caesar.
Artemidorus	:	A philosopher.
Octavius	:	Julius Caesar's heir and nephew.
Cinna	:	A poet.

JULIUS CAESAR

1

CHANGES IN ROME

Early in her history, *Rome* was ruled by a group of her noblest citizens. These formed the senate. The senate ruled wisely and well because its members worked for the public good. Later on, when Rome grew rich and powerful, the senate and the citizens grew selfish. They put their own interests before the public good. They split into parties under party leaders. Then there began a fierce struggle for power between these parties and their leaders.

At the time of this story, the two most powerful men in Rome were *Pompey* and *Julius Caesar*. Both were great generals and in command of large armies. Caesar defeated Pompey and so became the most powerful man in Rome. He was ambitious and it seemed that he would make himself king of the city and its vast empire. However, most Romans did not want a king. Their history had taught them that kings soon became tyrants. They wanted the old form of government which was more democratic. They were suspicious of Caesar and even ready to kill him in order to save the ancient liberty of their country.

2

THE SOOTHSAYER'S WARNING

After his victory over Pompey, Caesar returned to Rome in great triumph. There was a public holiday to celebrate his victory. Great crowds were waiting for the triumphal procession to pass by. People had climbed to roof-tops to catch a glimpse of the mighty Caesar. Not so long ago, they had done the same to catch a glimpse of the mighty Pompey, but Pompey was now forgotten. Now they had eyes and cheers only for great Caesar.

A great shout arose as Caesar passed through the *Arch of Triumph* and proceeded on his triumphal way. The leading citizens surrounded him. On his left was *Mark Antony* who had been his chief officer in many bloody battles. On his right was the noble *Brutus*, Caesar's most trusted friend and a senator whom every-one held in the highest honour. Among these leading citizens there were many who were Caesar's enemies. They feared Caesar's ambition. Some of them envied Caesar's greatness.

Treachery was in the air. And a soothsayer was there to foretell it. He pushed himself to the front of the crowd and shouted these memorable words:

"Caesar! Caesar! Beware the *Ides of March*!"

Twice he repeated his warning but nobody listened to him. Most people thought that he was mad. The procession passed on. It was making its slow way to the *Field of Mars* where, as was the custom, games were going to be held in honour of the victorious general.

3

BRUTUS AND CASSIUS

Brutus, who was anxious and in no mood for revelry, left the procession. By chance, he came upon an acquaintance, a senator like himself, named *Cassius*. Cassius had long been Caesar's enemy but he always pretended to be Caesar's friend. He soon found out that Brutus was anxious over Caesar. He feared that the people, at the public games, were going to offer Caesar the crown of kind. Caesar would gladly accept it. That would mean the beginning of tyranny and the end of freedom for Rome.

Cunning Cassius began to belittle Caesar and to do his best to turn Brutus against him. "The people," said Cassius, "look upon Caesar as a superman, as a god, in fact. But he is only a weak man like the rest of us. I remember," he went on, "how we were swimming one day in the *Tiber*.

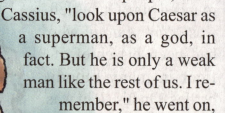

Caesar's strength gave out and he would have drowned if I hadn't been there to help him to the bank." Cassius then told Brutus other tales to show that Caesar was no better than anybody else. He ended with these words: "It is the duty of a noble Roman to prevent Caesar's being king and robbing Rome of her freedom."

4

BRUTUS' THOUGHTS

Brutus was the noblest of all the Romans and he could not bear the thought of tyranny and the slavery that comes with tyranny. The thought of Caesar's ambition had long troubled him. Now he realised that the time for action had come. He must act to save Rome. He must kill Caesar. He was Caesar's friend. He loved Caesar but he loved home more. He was ready to sacrifice his dearest friend for Rome. Such were Brutus' thoughts. He did not speak them aloud to Cassius, but when Cassius asked him what was to be done, he answered him, "I must think the matter over."

For some time, Brutus and Cassius talked together. Now and then, they caught the sounds of shouts and wild applause from the Field of Mars. Were the people offering to Caesar the crown of king? Was he accepting it? At last they saw the triumphal procession leaving the Field of Mars. A friend of Cassius's, named *Casca*, left the procession to join Brutus and Cassius. He was bringing them the news of what had happened at the games.

5

CASSIUS AIMS AT ENLISTING BRUTUS'S HELP

Casca reported that Caesar had been offered the crown of king by Mark Antony. Three times had Mark Antony offered it and three times had Caesar refused it. "But," said Casca, "Caesar refused it only because he was not certain that the crowd really wished it. He will accept it when it's offered to him again."

These words made Brutus more anxious than ever. He left  Cassius. Cassius went home to write some anonymous letters to Brutus. In these letters, he said that Rome was expecting Brutus to save the republic. When Casca came to visit Cassius, Cassius told him what he had done. He also told him that he was arranging a plot to kill Caesar. Casca readily agreed to join the plot. But, as both men knew, the plot could only succeed if Brutus joined it. Brutus was well-known for his honesty, and was respected by all men for his upright character. If he joined, many men would follow. All men would agree that their cause was just and honourable. Accordingly, Casca and Cassius decided to pay a visit to Brutus that very night. They would persuade him to join the plot.

That was the night before the Ides of March.

6

BRUTUS IS PERSUADED

That night, Brutus could not sleep. One thing was clear in his tormented mind. The life of the republic meant the death of Caesar. He felt he must put an end to Caesar before Caesar put an end to the republic. And yet, it was hard for him to kill his friend.

A servant brought in some anonymous letters which he had found in the window of his master's study. Brutus, high-minded Brutus, was easily deceived. He thought that different citizens had written the letters. All of them seemed to prove that the people of Rome were expecting him to save them from tyranny.

Soon after midnight, Cassius, Casca and other conspirators came to see Brutus. Cunning Cassius argued that it was Brutus' duty to save the republic. By such an argument he easily persuaded Brutus to join the plot. The details of the plot were then arranged. Caesar, they all agreed, was to be murdered in the senate-house that very morning. The conspirators wanted to kill Mark Antony as well but Brutus was against this. "Antony," he told them, "is but a limb of Caesar." Cassius warned Brutus that Mark Antony would be dangerous but Brutus refused to believe this. Unwillingly, the conspirators consented to let Mark Antony live.

Brutus' loving and loyal wife *Portia* had watched her husband anxiously all that evening. She saw that something

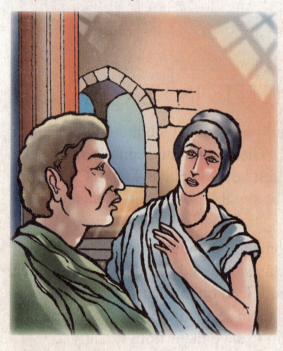

was weighing heavily on his mind. After midnight she heard her husband talking with several men. Who were those visitors who came so late and so secretly? When the visitors had left, she went to her husband.

"Tell me, I beg you, what is on your mind," she said to him. "I am your wife and I have the right to know what is troubling you." Brutus would have told her of the plot if another visitor had not arrived then. His wife's love and loyalty made Brutus all the more determined to kill Caesar. By so doing, he thought, he would become all the more worthy of her devotion.

7

CAESAR IGNORES CALPURNIA'S WARNINGS

In Caesar's house too, the night had been a troubled one. Caesar's wife *Calpurnia* had had terrible dreams. These, she said, were meant as a warning. Something dreadful was going to happen to Caesar. She begged him not to go out to the senate-house that day. The omens were all against it, she told him.

"I dreamt of a fierce battle in the sky," she said. "The noise of it shook the earth and drops of blood fell on the senate-house. I heard horses neighing, dying men groaning, and ghosts shrieking

in the streets. Something fearful is going to happen."

Caesar would not listen to his wife's fears. Nor would he listen to the augurers who sent him word that day was not favourable for Caesar to meet the senate. At this, Calpurnia begged him yet again not to go out. Caesar was about to obey her when *Decius*, one of the conspi-rators, came to accompany Caesar to the senate-house.

Caesar told Decius about one of Calpurnia's dreams. "She dreamed," he said, "that she saw my statue spouting blood and that hundreds of smiling Romans came to wash their hands in it." To Calpurnia this foretold Caesar's death. Decius, however, said that it foretold the opposite — that Rome would get fresh life from Caesar. The senate, he said, had decided to offer Caesar the crown that day. It would be folly to be absent because of a woman's dream.

Attracted by the thought of being made a king, Caesar then set out for the Capital, as the senate-house was called. His escort were the men who were going to murder him when he reached it!

8

THE MURDER

In the meantime, some rumours of the plot were spreading. *Artemidorus*, a philosopher who saw that anarchy would follow Caesar's death, did his best to warn Caesar. He wrote a letter of warning and he even named the chief conspirators. He was waiting in the street to present his letter to Caesar as he passed by on his way to the Capitol. As Caesar passed, Artemidorus held out his letter for him to take. Then Decius quickly pushed another

letter in front of it, and so Caesar had no chance to read Artemidorus's warning.

When Caesar reached the Capitol, one of the conspirators drew Mark Antony to one side as if to ask him something in private. A second conspirator presented Caesar with a petition in which pardon was asked for a banished senator. The other conspirators drew nearer as if they were anxious to speak in favour of the petition. Then, at a sign from Casca, they rushed forward and one by one they stabbed Caesar. Caesar staggered but stood upright till Brutus stabbed him. Then he fell dead, crying with his last breath, "Oh, Brutus! You too!"

9

CONFUSION

There followed a scene of confusion. The conspirators did not know what to do next. They did not know which way the crowd would turn. The senators who had been friendly towards Caesar trembled for their own safety. Then Brutus proclaimed that no one else would be killed and that only the conspirators were responsible for the death of Caesar. To pacify the people, Brutus suggested that he and the other conspirators should speak to the crowd in the market place. There they should give reasons for what they had done.

Mark Antony had fled to his house. But he now sent word that he was ready to consent to the death of Caesar if there was a good reason for it. High-minded Brutus sent a message to Mark Antony saying that he might safely leave his house. Antony did so. He boldly told the conspirators that they might kill him too, if they wished. This bold gesture won over Brutus who promised that he would be Antony's friend and see that he was safe. Furthermore, Brutus granted Antony's request to speak at Caesar's funeral. Cassius whispered to Brutus that allowing Antony to speak was dangerous. Antony was a powerful orator and he could win the people to his cause and turn them against the conspirators. Noble Brutus was too honest a man to suspect treachery and he did not listen to Cassius. Cassius, however, was right. Mark Antony was already at work to ruin the conspirators. He had already sent a message to *Octavius,* Caesar's nephew and heir, telling him what had happened and urging him to gather an army.

10

TWO SPEECHES

Meanwhile, the body of Caesar was carried to the public forum or market place. There Brutus spoke to the crowd. He gave his reasons for the murder of Caesar. "I killed Caesar because he was ambitious," he told them. "His ambition was driving him on to become king. I had to kill him to save our republic and our freedom. It is true that Caesar was my best friend but a man should be ready to kill his best friend for the good of Rome. Would you," he asked them "rather have Caesar alive and be slaves, or Caesar dead and be free men?" The crowd shouted its applause and Brutus went away, satisfied with his achievement. Before

he left, however, he begged the crowd to give a friendly hearing to Mark Antony's speech.

Mark Antony was indeed a most powerful orator. At first the people were against him but he was soon able to win them to his side. He did not appeal to their reason, as Brutus had done but, cunningly, he appealed to their feelings.

The conspirators, he told the mob, had accused Caesar of being ambitious. They were all honourable men, but was their charge really true? Caesar had spent a lot of money, not on himself, but on the people. He had been a true friend to the poor. Three times he had been offered the crown of king. Three times he had refused it. Was that ambition? "Yet Brutus says that he was ambitious," he said, "and Brutus is an honourable man."

The people were excited by these words. Then Mark Antony held out Caesar's will for all to see. "If you knew what Caesar had left you in his will, you would go and kiss dead Caesar's wounds; you would dip your handkerchiefs in his sacred blood and even beg a hair of him for memory."

By this time, the crowd was raging against the murderers. Mark Antony enraged them still further by pointing to the wounds in Caesar's body:

"See what a rent the envious Casca made!

Through this, the well-beloved Brutus stabbed.

This was the most unkindest cut of all."

Mark Antony then returned to the will — which, he said, he would not read for fear of exciting the crowd against those honourable men who had killed Caesar.

"The will! The will!" shouted the mob. "We want to hear the will!"

With pretended unwillingness, Mark Antony told them the contents of Caesar's will. Caesar had left a sum of money to every citizen of Rome. Besides that, he had left to them all his lands, his gardens and his orchards on the bank of the Tiber. There they could take their walks in the evening when their work was done. Mark Antony ended with a heartfelt cry:

"When will there ever be another man like Caesar?"

11

REIGN OF TERROR

Mark Antony had succeeded only too well. Wild with fury, the crowd ran here and there to kill the conspirators and burn their houses. On their way, they met a poet who unluckily had the same name as one of the conspirators. *Cinna* he was called. They attacked this poor Cinna

and cut him to pieces just because of his name.

Brutus and Cassius were warned in time and were able to flee from the city.

While Brutus and Cassius were fleeing through one gate of the city, Octavius and Mark Antony were entering the city through another. They were at the head of a large army. Soon, Octavius and Mark Antony made themselves masters of the city. All senators and citizens who had been against Caesar were instantly put to death. Indeed there was for a time a reign of terror. When this was over, Octavius and Mark Antony marched to attack Brutus and Cassius who were gathering together an army to recover Rome.

12

TWO SUICIDES

The enemies met in battle at *Philippi* in *Macedonia*. In that distant, eastern part of the Roman Empire, Brutus and Cassius, had been able to gather a fairly strong army. However, Brutus and Cassius were no longer friends. Cassius was too violent and unjust for Brutus. At the same time, Brutus was a philosopher rather than a practical man so that his decisions were often wrong.

They were certainly wrong at the battle of Philippi. There Brutus sent his troops against Octavius when he ought to have sent them to help Cassius against Mark Antony. The result was that Cassius's army was defeated and Cassius killed himself. The defeat of Cassius left Antony free to come to the help of Octavius who was being hard pressed by Brutus. Brutus's forces were defeated. Brutus was in despair. He realised that the murder of Caesar had not saved the republic but had led to senseless bloodshed. He thereupon committed suicide.

Thus ended the life of Brutus who so nobly sacrificed himself to save the freedom of his country. Mark Antony, after Brutus' death, spoke of him in this manner:

This was the noblest Roman of them all.

All the conspirators, save only he.
Did that they did in envy of great Caesar.
He only, in a general honest thought,
And common good to all, made one of them.
His life was gentle, and the elements
So mixed in him that nature might stand up
And say to all the world, "This was a man!"

OTHELLO

The People in the Story

Brabantio   : A rich senator of Venice.

Desdemona   : Brabantio's only daughter.

Othello   : A noble Moor from North Africa.

The Duke of Venice :

Iago   : One of Othello's officers, a wicked man.

Emilia   : Iago's wife.

Montano   : Governor of Cyprus.

Cassio   : Othello's second-in-command.

Barbary   : Maid of Desdemona's mother.

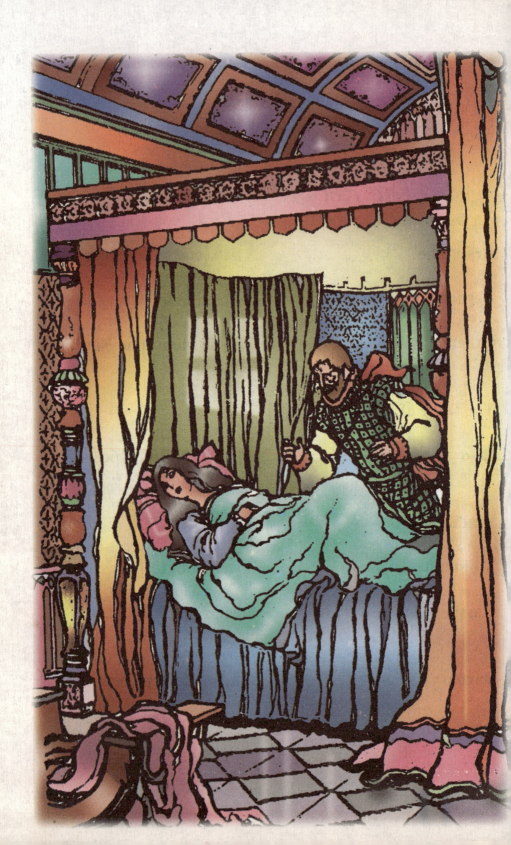

OTHELLO

1

A SECRET MARRIAGE

Brabantio, a rich senator of Venice, had only one child, a daughter named *Desdemona*. She was so beautiful that many young men of the best families wished to marry her. She refused them all because she loved *Othello*, a noble *Moor* from *North Africa*. Othello was a brave soldier who had risen to become a general. He had shown his bravery in many bloody battles against the *Turks*. Everyone praised him and the senate trusted and honoured him.

Brabantio often invited Othello to his house. There he and his daughter listened in wonder to Othello as he spoke about his adventures. Othello told them strange stories of battles he had fought in and places he had seen. He told them of deserts, caves and mountains high enough to touch the sky. He also told them of men who ate human flesh and of a strange race of people whose heads were under their shoulders.

Desdemona was fascinated by his stories and especially by the story of his life. This she found strange, wonderful and pitiful. Hearing it, she had to weep and yet she never tired of listening to it. She pitied Othello for the misfortunes and hardships of his life.

Her pity soon turned to love and she confessed to Othello that she loved him. Her beauty, gentleness and simplicity had already won the heart of Othello. One day, he begged her to marry him. Desdemona agreed to do so. But she had to marry Othello secretly, for she knew that her father would never consent to her marrying a Moor, a dark-skinned foreigner, no matter how noble he was by birth and character.

2

OTHELLO'S DEFENCE

Desdemona was right. Brabantio would never have consented to the marriage if he had known about it. But he had not known about it. He had left Desdemona free to choose her husband, thinking she would choose a noble *Venetian* as all the other high-born ladies of Venice did.

When Brabantio eventually heard of the marriage, he was furious. In the Senate, in front of the Duke, he accused Othello of stealing his daughter away from him by means of magic. This

was a grave accusation. By the law of Venice, it was a crime punishable by death.

The Senate, however, was in urgent need of Othello's services. A messenger had just brought the news that a Turkish fleet was on its way to attack *Cyprus* which, at that time, belonged to Venice. The Senate needed Othello to command the army against the Turks. They felt that the safety of Cyprus depended on Othello.

The Senate listened attentively to Brabantio's accusation, for they respected his age and his character. All the same they felt that the charge he had brought against Othello was wild and foolish. They summoned Othello to appear before them and listened to his defence.

Othello told them, "I will tell you plainly how I won my lady's love. Her father liked me and often invited me to his house. He asked me to tell him of my adventures. Little by little, I told him the story of my life. I told him how I had been taken prisoner by the enemy and sold as a slave. I told him of my exciting escape. A thousand such stories I told him again and again. Then one evening, when Desdemona and I were by ourselves, she begged me to tell her my life story from the beginning till now. She cried over my misfortunes. She loved me for the dangers I had met with, and I loved her because she pitied me for them. That is the only magic that I used to win my lady."

"I think that such tales would have won my daughter too," remarked the Duke.

3

OTHELLO WINS HIS CASE

Desdemona was then summoned before the senate.

"Answer me," cried out Brabantio, "am I not your father? Am I not the man you should obey?"

"Noble father," Desdemona answered him, "I owe you my life, my upbringing, and my love. That is my duty,

but I have a higher duty towards my husband. I owe him the same duty as my mother owed you."

Brabantio saw that he had lost his case. He said to Othello, "If I could take my daughter away from you, I would. But I see that I cannot. Take her then. I give you that which you have already won." Bitterly, he added, "I am glad that I have no other daughter. If I had, Desdemona's example would make me cruel to her." He added, "But beware! She has deceived her father, and she could just as easily deceive you."

Brabantio then turned to the Duke. "I beg you now, my lord, to go on with our business."

"The Turks are on their way to attack Cyprus," the Duke said to Othello. "You know the island well and we wish you to go there and take command. I'm afraid that you'll have to leave your wife behind you."

"Oh, my lord, let me go with him!" begged Desdemona.

"Let her come," said Othello. "Do not think that I shall neglect my duties when she is with me. On the contrary, she will help me. I need her company more than anything else. I am ready to leave at once, my lord. My officer *Iago* is a most honourable man whom I trust entirely. He will bring me your messages. Let my wife set sail after me in the care of the trusty Iago and his good wife *Emilia*."

"It shall be so," the Duke agreed.

Othello set sail at once. Desdemona began her preparations to follow him in the company of "trusty" Iago and his wife Emilia.

4

DESDEMONA ARRIVES IN CYPRUS

Montano, the governor of Cyprus, was anxiously looking out to sea where a fearful storm was raging. An anxious crowd was gathered on the shore. Everyone was asking: Would the Turks arrive before Othello and his troops?

Would all ships be wrecked in the terrible storm?

"What ship can hold together when such mountains of water fall on her?" asked Montano. "The Turkish ships can never live in such seas."

Cassio, who was Othello's second-in-command, arrived, bringing this news: "Most of the Turkish ships are sunk. Othello is still at sea. The fierce winds separated my ship from his." He gave a heartfelt cry, "Oh heaven preserve my master!"

Soon after, another messenger arrived with the news that Iago's ship had just reached harbour safely. "Ha!" exclaimed Cassio, "Even the storm bends before the beauty of Desdemona."

"Who is she?" Montano asked.

"The wife of Othello, too lovely to describe," Cassio told him.

It was not long before Desdemona reached the governor in his castle. "What news of my lord, Cassio?" Desdemona asked anxiously.

"He has not arrived yet. We are watching for his ship."

Desdemona was very anxious. She stood beside Cassio and took his hand for comfort. Cassio was an old friend of hers and of Othello's. He had helped Othello in his courtship of Desdemona and Desdemona was deeply grateful to him. She valued him as a friend but her whole heart was given to Othello.

"Trusty" Iago watched Desdemona and Cassio holding hands. His evil thoughts ran like this: "Ha! She's taking his hand. He's kissing her fingers. He's whispering in her ear. With little things like these, I'm going to catch him in my net."

5

IAGO'S EVIL PLAN

Actually, Iago was an evil man, and was not at all "trusty". He hated Othello because he envied him. He hated Cassio for the same reason. Othello had recently appointed Cassio as his second-in-command. Iago thought that he, as the older officer, should have been promoted to this rank instead of Cassio. Wild with envy, Iago was planning to ruin Othello and Cassio. If Desdemona was ruined too, it would make his triumph complete.

Iago planned to make Othello jealous and to drive him mad with jealousy. Cassio was much younger than Othello and he was Desdemona's country-man. He was hand-some, charming and very popular with the ladies. Iago was plan-ning to make Othello think that Desdemona loved Cassio in secret. There-fore, his wicked heart rejoiced at seeing Cassio and Desdemona holding hands.

There was a sudden shout: "A sail! A sail!"

Othello's ship had reached harbour safely!

Desdemona ran to meet the man whom she loved with all her heart. "Oh, my heart's joy!" she cried.

Othello kissed her, saying, "May our love increase as the days go by." Othello turned to the governor. "The war is over," he told him. "The storm has fought the battle for us. Our enemies are drowned."

He led Desdemona into the castle.

6

IAGO'S PLANS DEVELOP

The whole island rejoiced at the wrecking of the Turkish ships and the safe arrival of Othello and his troops. Cyprus was safe and the people made merry. There was feasting and revelry everywhere. The streets rang with shouts and laughter.

Cassio was in charge of the guard that night. Othello had given

him strict orders to keep the soldiers from getting drunk. Otherwise their drunken disorder might disgust the people and turn them against the rule of Venice.

Iago set to work to make Cassio drunk. At first Cassio refused to drink any wine. Little by little, however, one glass led to another and he was soon completely drunk. This was a bad example to the men under him. The cunning Iago then persuaded another officer to quarrel with Cassio. The two officers began to fight. When Montano, the governor, tried to stop them, Cassio wounded him.

Disorder and confusion spread among the officers and men. Iago secretly sent a man to ring the castle bell as if a dangerous mutiny had broken out instead of merely a drunken quarrel.

The ringing of the bell alarmed the city and awoke Othello. He rushed to the scene of the quarrel.

"Stop that bell," he commanded. "It will alarm the whole island." He turned to Iago, asking, "Honest Iago, tell me who began this."

Iago pretended to defend Cassio. However he spoke in such a way as to make Cassio's fault seem graver than it really was. Cunningly, he ended his story with these words, "But men are men; even the best sometimes forget."

Othello said to him, "I know your honesty, Iago. You're trying to make Cassio's wrong-doing seem less serious. But I must insist on strict discipline. Cassio, you will never more be an officer of mine."

7

IAGO'S SECOND TRICK

Iago's first trick had succeeded. His hated rival had lost his rank. Iago then planned his second trick. He went to visit Cassio, pretending that he had come to help him. Cassio was desperate with shame and remorse. "How ashamed of myself I am!" he exclaimed, adding, "Oh, God! That men should put an enemy in their mouths to steal away their brains."

Cunning Iago spoke to him thus, "Pah! Any man can get drunk now and then and no harm is done. I'll tell you what to do. Our general's wife is now the general. She can do what she likes with Othello. Ask her to beg Othello to give you back your rank. He'll do anything she asks him to."

Hearing this, Cassio began to look more cheerful. "That's a good idea," he told Iago. "I'll go to her early in the morning and ask her to help me. I'm sure she will. Thank you, honest Iago, for your good advice. You're a true friend."

"Honest!" Iago smiled to himself. His wicked plan seemed likely to succeed. Desdemona would beg Othello to forgive Cassio. Meanwhile, he would plant the seeds of jealousy in Othello's mind. Thus, Desdemona, in pleading for her friend, would seem to be pleading for her lover.

8
DESDEMONA FALLS INTO THE TRAP

Early the next morning, Cassio went to see Desdemona. "You may be sure, good Cassio, that I shall do all I can for you. I'll soon have you and my lord as friendly as ever. I'll speak to him in bed and at his meals. I won't let him rest till he has promised me what I ask. I would rather die than fail in helping you," she told him earnestly.

Cassio took her hand in gratitude.

Othello came in and saw them thus. Cassio went away at once. He was ashamed of himself and felt that he could not meet Othello face to face. But it looked as if he shared some guilty secret with Desdemona. Iago instantly seized the chance to make it seem so.

"I do not like this," he said.

"What did you say?" Othello asked him.

"Nothing, my lord."

"Wasn't that Cassio who went out as we came in?"

"Cassio? No, I don't think it was Cassio. Cassio wouldn't go away so furtively...."

"I believe it was Cassio."

In this way, Iago began to sow the seeds of jealousy in Othello's noble mind. These grew quickly because Othello believed that Iago was an honest man. Othello's nature was too noble for him to suspect evil in others.

9

STOKING THE FIRE OF JEALOUSY

Desdemona begged her husband to have pity on Cassio and to be friendly with him again. "Call him back. Speak to him. Promise me that you will," she begged.

"Not now, sweet Desdemona. Some other time."

"Tonight at supper?"

"No. Not tonight."

"Tomorrow at dinner?"

"I shall not be home for dinner."

"Then tomorrow night, or the day after, or the day after that? Name the time. Cassio is really very sorry for what he has done."

"Oh, let him come to me when he likes. Now leave me alone. I'm feeling tired."

It was jealousy, however, not tiredness, that weighed heavily on Othello. Cunning Iago warned him not to be jealous. "Guard against jealousy," he urged him. "The man who knows that his wife is unfaithful is unhappy. But the man who is only unsure about her is even more unhappy. Jealousy is a terrible thing. Men are jealous because they love, and jealousy destroys love."

"I know," said Othello, "that my wife is beautiful, loves company and feasting, sings, plays, and dances well, but I cannot be jealous of her because of that. I must have proof."

"And I have no proof," said Iago, with seeming honesty. "I may be quite wrong. I hope that I am. But watch her when she is with Cassio. I know the ladies of Venice better than you do. They're very clever at deceiving their husbands. After all, she deceived her father...."

He stopped. Othello in his mind finished his sentence, "and she could just as easily deceive me."

10
OTHELLO BECOMES MAD WITH JEALOUSY

From that moment, Othello knew no peace of mind. "She's deceiving me," he thought in despair. "My only hope lies in learning to hate her." He could not sleep. He could not rest. He lost all interest in war and soldiers. He was tormented by jealousy. Was his wife true to him? Sometimes he thought that she was. Sometimes he thought that she was not. Was Iago honest? He could not be sure. His doubt led him to seize Iago by the throat. "Give me proof of her guilt," he shouted wildly, "or I'll kill you for lying."

"I'm no liar," Iago answered him. "And if you want proof, I can give it to you. Didn't your wife have a handkerchief that was embroidered with a pattern of straw-berries?"

"She did. I gave it to her. It was my first gift to her."

"I saw Cassio wipe his mouth with it today."

"Blood! Blood! I will have their blood!" shouted Othello, mad with jealousy. "I will have my revenge on them."

"And I will give my mind, heart, and hands to the service of wronged Othello," swore Iago.

"Within three days, I want to hear that Cassio is dead," commanded Othello.

"You shall," promised Iago. "But let her live."

"No! Curse her! That beautiful witch shall die too!"

11

THE LOST HANDKERCHIEF

Desdemona had not given her handkerchief to Cassio. She had dropped it one day and Emilia, Iago's wife, had found it. Iago had taken it from her and had put it in Cassio's room.

Othello, in order to rest his wife, pretended that he had a headache. "Lend me your handkerchief to tie round my head," he asked Desdemona.

Desdemona held out her handkerchief.

"No, not that one. The one I gave you."

"I.... I can't find it."

"What! A gipsy gave that handkerchief to my mother. She told her that my father would love her as long as she kept it. If she lost it or gave it away, she would lose my father's love. When my mother

was dying, she gave it to me for my wife. I did so, as you know."

"Oh dear!" whispered Desdemona in fear. She feared that she had lost her husband's love with the handkerchief. She hid her fears and said, "You're making this up to prevent my asking you again about Cassio. You are going to pardon him, aren't you?" Then she began to praise Cassio. Othello left the room angrily.

Desdemona was bewildered by his strange behaviour. "Can he be jealous?" she asked herself. But then she grew angry with herself for thinking so badly of her noble husband. "Men are not gods," she said. "We must not expect such gentleness from them when they are married as they show us on the wedding day."

12

DESDEMONA IS DISTURBED

One day, Othello told Desdemona to her face that she was false.

"How can you say that?" his lady gently answered. "With whom am I false?"

Othello wept. "You have broken my heart, Desdemona. You are as false as you are beautiful. I wish that you had never been born."

Again he left angrily, leaving Desdemona filled with wonder at her lord's strange accusation. Suddenly she felt tired out. She began to hum a little tune, explaining to her attendant, Emilia, "My mother had a maid called *Barbary*. She was in love with a man but the man left her. She sang a song about a willow-tree and she died while singing it. I can't get that song out of my mind." As if in a dream, the poor lady then began to sing Barbary's song, "Willow, willow, willow." She told Emilia that she wanted to sleep for she was feeling very tired. After a moment, she said, "Oh, these men! These men! Do you think there are women who treat their husbands so cruelly?"

"Yes," Emilia answered her, "there are some, but I think it is all the fault of their husbands. Let them treat us properly or let them take the consequences!"

"Good night, Emilia," Desdemona said. "Oh, God, let my suffering make me better, not worse," she prayed.

13

END OF A GREAT LOVE

Desdemona was sleeping a troubled sleep when Othello came in to kill her. He looked down at her by the light of his candle. He thought, "I will not stain her white skin with blood. But she must die or she will ruin me. I'll put out the light. If I put out this light, I can light it again. When I have picked a rose, I cannot give it life and growth again. It must die."

Othello kissed Desdemona again and again. "Once more," he said, "and this will be the last."

Desdemona woke up.

She looked at Othello and saw him roll his eyes and bite his lower lip. She knew then that he meant to kill her.

"Have you said your prayers?"

"Yes, my lord."

"Pray that your sins be forgiven you. I will kill your body but not your soul."

"Oh, my lord, what is the matter?"

"You gave that handkerchief to Cassio."

"No, my lord, on my life and soul, I did not. Send for him and ask him."

"Do not tell lies. You are on your death-bed. I saw him with your handkerchief."

"Then he found it. I did not give it to him. Ask him."

"He's dead. I commanded Iago to kill him."

"What? Is he dead? Oh, poor Cassio!"

"Do you weep for him in front of me? You shall die."

"Kill me tomorrow. Let me live tonight!"

"No!"

"Only half an hour — while I say one prayer."

"It's too late."

"Oh, Lord! Lord!"

Othello pressed her pillow hard on her face and held it there till she was suffocated!

14

TRAGEDY UPON TRAGEDY

When Emilia returned to see if her mistress was asleep, she found her dead. Othello was standing beside the bed with his face twisted in anguish.

"She's dead. I've killed her," he told Emilia. "I killed her because she was false to me. Honest Iago has told me all."

Emilia knew that her husband was not honest at all. Indeed she had long suspected him of making trouble between Othello and her mistress. And then she screamed, "Murder! Help! The Moor has killed my lady! Help!"

Montano and Iago came running in.

"Iago, your lies have caused this murder," Emilia said.

"Be silent, woman!" Iago ordered her sharply.

"I will not be silent. I see it all now. Oh, foolish Moor, my lady did not give Cassio that handkerchief. I found it and my husband took it from me. He had begged me time and time again to steal it from my lady."

It was only then that Othello understood Iago's wickedness. With a terrible cry, he drew his sword, meaning to kill Iago. Montano managed to hold him back. While the two men were struggling, Iago stabbed Emilia with his dagger and ran away, for he saw that his brief triumph was over.

"Oh, lay me by my lady's side," gasped Emilia with her dying breath. "Oh, Moor, she was good. She loved you truly."

"I know. I see it all now," Othello said hoarsely. Lifting his sword, he drove it through his own body. "Here is my journey's

end," he gasped, as he fell on the bed where his lady lay. He kissed her cold lips once more before he died.

Iago did not escape punishment. He was soon caught. By order of the senate of Venice, he was put to death after undergoing the most fearful torture.

Thus ends the tragedy of Othello, the truly noble Moor, who loved not wisely but too well.

QUESTIONS

Use direct speech rather than indirect speech in your answers whenever possible.

AS YOU LIKE IT

1. (1) Who was Duke Frederick?
   (2) How did Duke Senior live in the Forest of Arden?
   (3) What do you know about (a) Rosalind? (b) Celia?

2. (1) What happening changed the life of the two girls?
   (2) Why did Rosalind pity the young man?

3. (1) What do you know about Orlando?
   (2) What had Oliver done before the wrestling match?
   (3) What had Charles promised Oliver?

4. (1) What made Duke Frederick very angry?
   (2) What did Rosalind give to Orlando?
   (3) Who fell in love at first sight?

5. (1) Why did Orlando leave the court immediately?
   (2) What made Duke Frederick banish Rosalind?

6. (1) Who was going to share Rosalind's banishment?
   (2) Where did the two girls decide to go?
   (3) How did Rosalind and Celia disguise themselves?
   (4) What new names did the two girls take?

7. (1) What warning did Adam give Orlando?
   (2) How did Adam show his goodness?
   (3) Where did Orlando and old Adam wander to?

8. (1) What did Rosalind ask the two shepherds?
   (2) What did the kindly shepherd say?
   (3) What did the two girls buy?

9. (1) What happened to old Adam in the forest?
   (2) What made Duke Senior tell Orlando, "Your manners are very bad."?
   (3) How did Duke Senior help Orlando and his servant?

10. (1) What astonished the two girls?
    (2) Who was the poet and lover?
    (3) What did Rosalind invite Orlando to do?
    (4) What question did Duke Senior ask Ganymede and what answer did Ganymede give?

11. (1) Whom did Orlando come upon one day?
    (2) In what danger was Oliver?
    (3) What dreadful thought came into Orlando's mind?
    (4) What did Orlando do?

12. (1) What made Oliver become "a truly loving brother"?
    (2) Why had Oliver come to the forest?
    (3) What did Orlando send to Ganymede?
    (4) When did Ganymede nearly faint?

13. (1) What surprising news did Oliver tell Orlando?
    (2) What did Orlando say when he heard the news?
    (3) What did Rosalind tell Orlando?

14. (1) What question did Ganymede ask (a) Duke Senior? (b) Orlando?
    (2) When were Duke Senior and Orlando overjoyed?
    (3) What made the forest "ring with revelry"?

(4) What good news was brought to Duke Senior?
(5) How does the story end?

THE TEMPEST

1. (1) What do you know about (a) Prospero? (b) Miranda?
   (2) Who were (a) Ariel? (b) Sycorax? (c) Caliban?
2. (1) What did Miranda beg her father to do?
   (2) Why had Prospero raised that fearful storm?
   (3) What did Miranda remember of her life before she came to the island?
3. (1) What did Prospero tell Miranda about his former life?
   (2) How had Antonio tried to kill Prospero and Miranda?
   (3) Who had saved the lives of Prospero and his daughter?
   (4) Who were travelling on the ship?
   (5) What news was Ariel bringing to his master?
4. (1) Where was the son of the King of Naples?
   (2) What made Prospero say of Ferdinand, "My daughter must see him."?
   (3) What had happened to Antonio and the King of Naples?
   (4) What will Prospero do if Ariel obeys his commands?
   (5) Where did Ariel lead Ferdinand?
5. (1) What did Miranda exclaim when she first saw Ferdinand?
   (2) What did Ferdinand take Miranda for?
   (3) Why did Prospero treat Ferdinand harshly?
   (4) What did Miranda say to her father when he seemed so unkind?
6. (1) What hard task had Ferdinand to perform?
   (2) What did Miranda beg Ferdinand?
   (3) Where was Prospero while Miranda and the prince were talking together?
   (4) What would Ferdinand be one day?
   (5) When did Prospero appear before the lovers?
   (6) How will Prospero make up for his unkindness?
7. (1) What had Ariel done to make Antonio and his ally repent?
   (2) How did Ariel draw the repentant men to Prospero's cave?
   (3) What did Antonio and his ally promise Prospero?
   (4) What did Prospero mean when he said, "I have something to give you too."?
   (5) Why must the King of Naples ask Miranda to forgive him?
8. (1) What words made Antonio weep for shame?
   (2) What made Gonzalo weep?
   (3) What astonished the guests in the cave?
   (4) What did Prospero do before he left the enchanted island?
   (5) What was the song that Ariel sang?

MACBETH

1. (1) Who was Macbeth?
   (2) Who was returning from the battle-field with Macbeth?
   (3) Who suddenly appeared before the two commanders?
   (4) How did the third witch hail Macbeth?
   (5) What did the third witch say to Banquo?
2. (1) How had the witches' first prophecy come true?
   (2) What thought was in Macbeth's mind when he told Banquo, "Now you can hope that your descendants will become kings."?
   (3) What did Banquo say about the witches?
   (4) Why did Macbeth rejoice over the witches' prophecy?
3. (1) What was Lady Macbeth determined to do?
   (2) Why was Lady Macbeth sure that her husband would hesitate to kill the king?
   (3) When would they murder King Duncan?

4. (1) What reason had Macbeth for not killing the king?
   (2) What made Lady Macbeth call her husband "a coward"?
   (3) How did Lady Macbeth further tempt her husband?
5. (1) How did Macbeth silence the royal guards?
   (2) What prevented Lady Macbeth from killing the king?
   (3) What terrible vision did Macbeth see?
   (4) Did the vision prevent Macbeth from murdering Duncan?
   (5) What made Macbeth stop before leaving the King's room?
6. (1) What voice did Macbeth seem to hear?
   (2) Why did Lady Macbeth return to Duncan's room?
   (3) (a) Why was Macbeth gazing at his hands?
       (b) What question was he asking as he gazed at them?
7. (1) What made Macbeth "tremble like a leaf"?
   (2) What did Lady Macbeth urge her husband to do?
   (3) How did Macbeth pretend to show his loyalty to the dead king?
   (4) What made the king's sons flee?
   (5) How was the witches' second prophecy fulfilled?
8. (1) Why did Macbeth determine to kill Banquo and his son?
   (2) How did Macbeth arrange the murder of Banquo and Fleance?
   (3) Did the murderers succeed in killing the two men?
   (4) How did the witches' prophecy about Banquo come true?
9. (1) What appeared in the chair reserved for Banquo?
   (2) What made the guests wonder what was the matter with their host?
   (3) What sent Macbeth "quite out of his mind"?
   (4) How did Lady Macbeth explain her husband's strange behaviour?
   (5) Were the guests satisfied with her explanation?
   (6) Why did Macbeth decide to consult the three witches?
10. (1) What strange mixture were the witches cooking in their kettle? Why?
    (2) What did the three ghosts look like?
    (3) What did the three ghosts say to Macbeth?
    (4) What answer did the witches give to Macbeth's question: "Will Banquo's descendants reign in Scotland?"?
11. (1) What fearful revenge did Macbeth take on Macduff?
    (2) What made Macbeth wish that he were dead?
    (3) What drove Lady Macbeth to kill herself?
12. (1) What did Macbeth do when he heard that his enemies were advancing?
    (2) What gave Macbeth strength to resist?
    (3) What strange news did the messenger bring to Macbeth?
    (4) Explain how Birnam Wood was able to march to Dunsinane.
    (5) Who was determined to kill Macbeth? Why?
    (6) Why did Macbeth tell Macduff that he was wasting his blows?
    (7) How did Macduff answer Macbeth?
    (8) What happened to Macbeth at the end of the story?

A MIDSUMMER NIGHT'S DREAM

1. (1) What was the "cruel law" in Athens?
   (2) What did Egeus complain about?
   (3) How did Hermia defend herself?
   (4) What was the verdict of Duke Theseus?
2. (1) What did Lysander urge Hermia to do?
   (2) Whom did the lovers tell of their intention?
   (3) What did Helena do when she heard of the lovers' intention?
3. (1) What do you know about the wood where the lovers were going to meet?
   (2) What was the cause of the quarrel between the fairy king and queen?
   (3) What was Oberon's threat to Titania?

4. (1) What do you know about Puck?
   (2) What command did Oberon give to Puck?
   (3) What was Oberon going to do with the magic flower?
   (4) When would Oberon take the spell off Titania?

5. (1) What did Oberon overhear?
   (2) What made Oberon pity Helena?
   (3) What did Oberon command Puck to do to Demetrius?
   (4) How will Puck recognise Demetrius?

6. (1) Where did Oberon find Titania?
   (2) What commands was Titania giving to her fairies?
   (3) What did Oberon do with the love-juice?

7. (1) Where were Hermia and Lysander?
   (2) What made Puck think that Lysander was Demetrius?
   (3) Whom did Lysander see when he awoke?
   (4) What made Helena think that Lysander was making a fool of her?
   (5) What did Lysander do when Helena ran away?

8. (1) What did Hermia do when she awoke?
   (2) What did Oberon do when he found Demetrius?
   (3) Whom did Demetrius see when he awoke?
   (4) How did Demetrius address Helena?

9. (1) What astonished Hermia?
   (2) What did Helena say to Hermia?
   (3) What did the two men do while the two ladies were quarrelling?

10. (1) Who had heard the lovers quarrelling?
    (2) What did Oberon command Puck to do?
    (3) Where did Oberon go?

11. (1) What did Oberon put over Bottom's head?
    (2) With whom did Titania fall in love?
    (3) Give the names of four fairies.
    (4) What did Titania order her fairies to do?

12. (1) What did Bottom ask Pease-blossom to do?
    (2) What did he order Cobweb to do?
    (3) What command did he give to Mustard-seed?
    (4) What did Bottom want to eat?
    (5) Where did Bottom fall asleep?

13. (1) What made Titania give the boy to Oberon?
    (2) How did Oberon release Titania from the magic spell?
    (3) What was Titania astonished at?
    (4) What did Oberon do to Bottom?
    (5) Where did Oberon take Titania?

14. (1) What had Puck done to Lysander?
    (2) Whom does Lysander now love?
    (3) With whom is Demetrius in love?
    (4) What did the lovers plan to do?

15. (1) Why had Theseus come to the forest?
    (2) What did Theseus think was "a happy end to the story"?
    (3) Did Egeus give his consent to the marriage of Hermis and Lysander?
    (4) How did the fairies celebrate the happy end?

JULIUS CAESAR

1. (1) How was Rome ruled early in her history?
   (2) What happened when Rome grew rich and powerful?
   (3) Who was the most powerful man in Rome at the time of this story?
   (4) Why were many citizens suspicious of Julius Caesar?

2. (1) How did Caesar enter Rome?
   (2) Who was
       (a) Mark Antony?
       (b) Brutus?
   (3) What was the soothsayer's warning?
3. (1) Why was Brutus anxious?
   (2) What do you know of Cassius?
   (3) What did Cassius try to do?
   (4) What was the duty of a noble Roman, according to Cassius?
4. (1) What were Brutus' thoughts?
   (2) What did Brutus and Cassius hear as they were talking?
   (3) What did they fear was happening in the Field of Mars?
   (4) What did Casca come to tell them?
5. (1) Had Caesar been offered the crown of king?
   (2) Had he accepted it?
   (3) What was in the letters that Cassius wrote?
   (4) Why must Brutus join the conspirators?
   (5) When were Cassius and Casca going to visit Brutus?
6. (1) What thing was clear in Brutus' tormented mind?
   (2) What did the letters seem to show?
   (3) How did Cassius persuade Brutus to join the conspiracy?
   (4) When would they murder Caesar?
   (5) Were the conspirators going to kill Mark Antony too?
   (6) What made Brutus even more determined to kill Caesar?
7. (1) What had Calpurnia dreamed?
   (2) What message did the augurers send?
   (3) Who persuaded Caesar to go to the senate-house? What did he say?
   (4) Who accompanied Caesar to the Capitol?
8. (1) What do you know about Artemidorus?
   (2) Describe how the conspirators murdered Caesar.
9. (1) What had Mark Antony done after the murder?
   (2) What did Brutus promise Mark Antony?
   (3) How was Mark Antony working against the conspirators?
10. (1) What did Brutus say to the people?
    (2) What did Mark Antony say?
    (3) What were the terms of Caesar's will?
    (4) Why did Mark Antony's speech please the people more than Brutus?
11. (1) What was the result of Mark Antony's speech?
    (2) What happened to Brutus and Cassius?
    (3) How did Mark Antony and Octavius make themselves masters of Rome?
12. (1) What caused the unfriendliness between Brutus and Cassius?
    (2) What mistake did Brutus make at Philippi?
    (3) Why was Brutus in despair?
    (4) How did Mark Antony speak of Brutus?

OTHELLO

1. (1) What do you know of Desdemona?
   (2) What made Desdemona and her father "listen in wonder" to Othello?
   (3) What made Desdemona fall in love with Othello?
   (4) Why had Desdemona to marry Othello secretly?
2. (1) What "grave accusation" did Brabantio bring against Othello?
   (2) Why was the senate in urgent need of Othello's services?
   (3) What was the "magic" that Othello had used to win Desdemona?
   (4) What did the Duke of Venice remark about Othello's "magic"?

3. (1) What did Desdemona tell her father?
   (2) What did Brabantio say to Othello?
   (3) What did the duke command Othello to do?
   (4) What do you know about Iago?
4. (1) What was making the governor of Cyprus so anxious?
   (2) (a) Who was Montano?
       (b) What good news did he bring?
       (c) What did he say about Desdemona?
   (3) What were Iago's thoughts when he saw Cassio and Desdemona holding hands?
5. (1) What do you now know about Iago?
   (2) How was Iago going to ruin Othello, Cassio and Desdemona?
   (3) Describe the meeting of Othello and Desdemona.
   (4) What good news did Othello bring to the governor?
6. (1) What caused the merry-making in Cyprus?
   (2) What orders had Othello given Cassio?
   (3) Why did Iago make Cassio drunk?
   (4) What was the result of Cassio's drunken behaviour?
7. (1) What did Cassio mean when he said, "Oh God, that men should put an enemy into their mouths to steal away their brains!"?
   (2) What was Iago's advice to Cassio?
   (3) Did Iago intend to help Cassio or to ruin him?
8. (1) What did Desdemona promise Cassio?
   (2) How were Desdemona and Cassio standing when Othello came in?
   (3) What did Othello think when Cassio went away furtively?
   (4) How did Iago sow the seeds of jealousy in Othello's mind?
   (5) What made these seeds grow fast?
9. (1) What did Iago say about jealousy?
   (2) What did Iago tell Othello to do?
   (3) How did Othello finish Iago's sentence beginning, "After all, she deceived her father...."?
10. (1) What robbed Othello of his peace of mind?
    (2) What proof did Iago give of Desdemona's guilt?
    (3) What has Iago to do within three days?
    (4) Is Othello going to kill Desdemona?
11. (1) How had Desdemona's handkerchief come into Cassio's possession?
    (2) What did Othello tell Desdemona about that handkerchief?
    (3) What made Othello rush out of the room "like a madman"?
    (4) What did Desdemona say to excuse Othello's strange behaviour?
12. (1) What did Othello tell Desdemona to her face?
    (2) What did Desdemona answer?
    (3) How did Desdemona feel after her husband's accusation? What did she do?
    (4) What did Desdemona say in her prayer?
13. (1) What were Othello's thoughts as he gazed on Desdemona asleep?
    (2) When did Desdemona know that Othello was going to kill her?
    (3) What did Desdemona tell Othello about the handkerchief?
    (4) What did Othello say had happened to Cassio?
    (5) How did Othello kill Desdemona?
14. (1) What did Emilia find?
    (2) What had Emilia long suspected?
    (3) What did Emilia tell
        (a) Iago?
        (b) Othello?
    (4) Why was Othello ready to kill Iago?
    (5) Why did Iago kill Emilia?
    (6) How did Othello die? What were his last words?
    (7) How was Iago punished?